Seven Conversations With Jerry

Seven
Conversations
with
Jerry

A Book about the Human Soul, Bereavement,
and the Afterlife

Rabbi Avraham E. Plotkin

Best Regards,

Rabbi. Avraham E. Plotkin

04/28/22

Ufarazta Press   NEW YORK | TORONTO

Published by Ufarazta Press

287 Hicks Street
Brooklyn NY 11201

83 Green Lane
Thornhill, Ontario L3T 6K6, Canada
www.chabadmarkham.org
info@chabadmarkham.org

ISBN: 978-0-578-74593-0

Printed in Bulgaria.

Type Composition by John Bernstein

Contents

Dedication

Dedicated to Zalmy (Boruch Schneur Zalman Plotkin), *a"h*, our beautiful, special son who passed away in April, 2018, two days before he would have turned age 15. Zalmy died so young, but he taught us much more about life than some of our greatest teachers!

We never realized how this book would turn out to be a source of comfort in our own time of need.

Foreword

The ironies of life. While finishing up this book, which I wrote to help those suffering a loss in their lives, I lost my own son. He was our youngest child and his name was Zalmy. He had Down's syndrome.

While Zalmy was, at times, a handful, he was the sweetest boy, huggable, and beloved. My wife, Goldie, and I became very attached to him and we loved him with all our heart and soul. His siblings adored him. Our community loved him. Anyone who got to know Zalmy found him endearing and unforgettable.

As you can surely imagine, when we received the tragic news that our otherwise healthy, beloved fourteen-year-old mysteriously passed away one morning, we were totally heartbroken.

Here I was, a rabbi, busy every day offering comfort to the whole world, and—now that my own heart was ripped to shreds—I had no one to turn to. I felt helpless. I could help others, but I couldn't figure out how to help myself. I was trapped in a dark place with no hope in sight.

Until…one day I started reading this book, *my own book*, and it was like magic. I was suddenly being helped. It was like being admitted into therapy and seeing the light! It was my own therapy this time, and I was both the patient and the therapist!

I felt that G–d had prepared, through me, the cure before our ailment struck. The comforting ideas of my own book were "like cold water to a faint soul," and they helped me redeem myself from some of my darkest moments!

The Inspiration

So, what inspired me in the first place—a rabbi of a large community synagogue in Toronto—to write yet another book about mourning and death?

It happened to me while visiting hundreds if not thousands of people mourning the loss of their loved ones. I made a startling discovery: I noticed that there were barely any books or resources addressing the burning ultimate issues associated with the loss of a loved one.

While there were numerous books that dealt with the traditions associated with death and mourning—and even a few noteworthy self-help books that addressed the psychological trauma experienced by mourners—there were almost none that dealt with the core ultimate issues.

Over the years, whenever I spoke to mourners after losing a loved one they would tell me how they were desperately searching for some answers, how they felt like they were groping in the dark, and how they can't even find a most basic book that addresses their issues.

I am talking here about macro issues like:

- Who says there is a soul?
- Does the soul live on posthumously without a body?
- Does the soul keep its personality and familial relations in the afterlife?
- Is there a Heaven and a Hell?
- How do we make sense of the seemingly senseless suffering in this world?
- How do we reconnect with the dead?
- Is there something we can do to help our deceased loved ones in their transition to the hereafter? and finally,
- How can we make a meaningful legacy for them down here on earth?

These are all questions that every mourner has to deal with, and these are the same questions that all of us will need to face up to, at one time or another in our lives.

In general, because these issues are extremely complex and not easy to resolve, people are afraid to confront them. It makes them feel inadequate. They fear confronting these Big Questions because it naturally causes them a great deal of embarrassment: Here they are, grown adults with many academic degrees, and they haven't even begun to figure out some of the most elementary issues about life and death! So, instead of dealing with the issues, they choose to preoccupy themselves for most of their lives with trivial matters where they can feel a false sense of security, like hanging out on computers and iPhones, managing the food they eat and the clothing they wear while—at all costs —avoiding confronting the real issues of life and death.

Yet, no matter how much they avoid these issues, there are moments that are crossroads in one's life, such as after the loss of a loved one, when they are forced to sit down and rethink these issues, reexamine their previous assumptions and renavigate life based on their new conclusions.

And when these matters finally do catch up to them in these vulnerable moments and they wrestle with the issues, they desperately need some guidance and direction. They need someone to hold their hand and to lead them. They need a book or a mentor to help them along on this bumpy journey, to guide them through these complicated issues.

So, in response to this gaping hole in the world of bereavement literature and in solidarity with my grieving brothers and sisters, I have girded my loins to take on this mammoth and monumental task and write this badly needed book. Over an extended period of close to ten years, I have collected, organized, and edited what I considered to be the most important and user-friendly ideas out there to help people make their transition in their time of need and to give them a better understanding of the soul and the afterlife.

While this book is mostly from Jewish sources, I would consider its main thoughts universal, as they echo the universal spiritual tradition.

This book is also very much in tune with the times and cognizant of the reality that people these days just don't have the time and patience to read a complete book, let alone some scholarly thesis about death and the afterlife. It's just a nonstarter!

That's why, when contemplating the format of this book, we were very careful to make the information appealing and engaging. Moreover, we prepared it in a story format that reads easily. We all know that people just love a good story!

Furthermore, instead of the expected sermon-style presentations, the ideas discussed by the rabbi in our story are clothed in engaging dialectic conversations in the tradition of the Talmud and the ancient Greeks—again to make some very scholarly ideas easier to digest and to remember!

One will hopefully find reading this book helpful and meaningful. It covers all the big issues from many angles, and, after reading this book, it should provide some true inner satisfaction and peace of mind! Because the subject matter is very broad, this book is by no means exhaustive. Its goal, however, is to give some meaningful comfort and general direction while at the same time whetting the reader's appetite to study more.

It is my prayerful hope that the ideas shared in this book resonate with the reader's soul, as the ideas shared are mostly from "real deal" authentic sources. They are culled from the Torah and Kabbalah. They are also based on many classes that I have given online over the years, which have helped me hone and fine-tune the content of this book, based on helpful feedback from many people across the globe!

The advice that the rabbi character offers in this book is not coming from a rabbinic ivory tower; rather, it is based on down-to-earth experiences in the field, taken from my personal exposure to real people as their rabbi.

We have also added, at the end of the book, a list of "Jerry's Questions," to help summarize the conversations with the rabbi and to facilitate group discussions. For the reader's further research, we have compiled a list of basic sources for all the subjects covered, as well as a glossary of all Hebrew terms used.

May this book succeed in bringing some further clarity to those who are experiencing bereavement as well as those who are simply travelling on life's journey and searching for a more meaningful life.

Rabbi Avraham E. Plotkin
Markham/Toronto, Ontario
Summer 2020

Note to the Reader:

Throughout this book, "G–d" is written with a dash instead of an "o." According to Torah law, the divine name is sacred, and great care must be taken to accord it proper care and reverence. For this reason, it is best to avoid writing or printing the word "G–d" in its full spelling lest it be unwittingly defaced or treated irreverently.

Animation:
How Do We Know There Is A Soul?

The sun dropped beneath the horizon as my car pulled into the long and winding driveway of Jerry Goldstein's magnificent mansion. Jerry had just lost his father and I was at a loss of what to tell him.

While bereavement was an integral part of my job as a rabbi and I had honed my comforting skills over the years to a fine art, I knew this was not going to be your average call. Jerry's relationship with his father had deteriorated over the last few years, and I worried that Jerry was going to have a hard time dealing with his father's death.

Worst of all, Jerry did not like me. I was his father's rabbi, not his, and the close relationship I had developed with Jerry's father since I'd moved to Ottawa over thirty years ago seemed to bother Jerry. I had watched the relationship between father and son crumble. The father-son duo had built the family business Morris started, and then had a falling out over ties with a shady company with an anti-Semitic past. Money was lost, but even sadder was the silence that had reigned between Morris and his only son.

My neck strained as I turned off my car, uncomfortable to face this middle-aged orphan. Unfortunately, Jerry blamed his father's religious fervor—that passion that had struck down the billion-dollar deal and had motivated Morris's Jewish charitable decisions—on me.

I usually avoided Jerry if I saw him in the supermarket, telling myself that I was being polite by staying out of the Goldstein family fight. But I couldn't abandon Jerry in this moment of loss. I had to be a peacemaker, even if Jerry didn't want to make peace with me. I knew that was what Morris would have wanted. He had told me this, days before he succumbed to cancer. I took a deep breath and hoped my years of training would kick in.

When I walked into the spacious, luxurious living room, I saw Jerry sitting on the floor. He looked shocking. It was like the lights in his eyes had turned off. The charismatic business executive who was always upbeat looked dismally depressed. He slowly gazed up through his baggy, sleep-deprived, blue eyes. I met his gaze, worried.

"Rabbi Goldberg," Jerry said feebly. "Thanks again for the meaningful service and thoughtful eulogy you gave in my father's honor. I know that Dad would have appreciated what you said about him."

I nodded, trying to hide my surprise. In the thirty years I had known Jerry, he had never greeted me warmly. He looked and sounded like a different person, a softer Jerry than the man I had come to know. I sat down beside him, knowing that at this point comforting was an impossible task in any circumstance, let alone with Jerry. "Don't comfort the mourner when the wound is still fresh," my rabbis taught me. "Let the mourner speak first." I knew that sitting in silence would be most appropriate, but it was awkward.

"You knew my father well," continued Jerry slowly, stroking his reddish grey beard with his manicured fingers. "He really liked you, Rabbi."

Jerry leaned forward. "But we both know how my father struggled with me," he confided in a whisper. "I can't believe he's gone." He held his head in his hands, covering his eyes. Jerry had always seemed invincible in his power suits — fit and confident. Now his voice was weak with grief, and his body hunched vulnerably in the low chair he sat on.

Was a nod enough to show Jerry I was there to support him?

Jerry motioned me closer and continued to speak. "My dad was what you would call a good man, a strong believer, despite all the hell he lived through. But as for me, it's a different story. You know I am not much of a believer. My father could never understand me. He provided a comfortable life for my mom and me, but he was so distant. I could not get close to him. I appreciate your coming, but there's not much to say."

I nodded in understanding. Indeed, Morris was my hero. I was so impressed with him. Here was a Holocaust survivor who always managed to project a positive disposition. I never once heard him complain. After witnessing the most horrifying and gruesome scenes in history, Morris went on to successfully and happily rebuild his life. And I owed my life to him. Ever since I'd taken the position of rabbi in Ottawa, away from my parents and family in New York, Morris had acted like my adoptive father.

My children loved Morris at least as much as I did. In their eyes, Morris sometimes even outranked their own father, especially in synagogue. I was the one in charge of shushing their antics, while Morris always had a stash of candies in his pocket, which he gladly and lovingly shared with my kids and with every child in our synagogue. Morris became affectionately known to all the children as the "candy man." To watch him bend down and pass out lollipops and Fizzers to small, hopeful faces was an absolute treat!

My children, having the special distinction of being the rabbi's children, received special attention from Morris, always receiving the best candies in his stash. I remember him calling out in his Eastern European Yiddish accent, "*Boy-ehs*, Goldberg *Boy-ehs*, come over for your candy. They are kosher: don't *vorry!*" My boys would be there in a flash. Then Morris would dig deep into his pocket to extract half-melted sweets and give it to my boys' outstretched hands, as they begged for more.

Losing Morris was painful for me too.

"You know, Rabbi," Jerry said, interrupting my quiet reverie, "when I stood in the cemetery this afternoon, looking into the grave, watching them lower my father's casket with his emaciated, cancer-riddled body into the cold ground with the worms and maggots, it shook me that his life had ended, finished, kaput, no more."

I leaned forward in what I hoped was a sympathetic gesture. I had never shared much more than a hockey update or joke with Jerry. I wanted to show him I was there to support him in his time of sorrow. I didn't think it was yet time to share my own warm moments of his father. Jerry needed a hug.

I gently placed my arm around Jerry and held tight. Like his dad, he had a small stocky build, so I was able to surround him in my long arms. Still, I had this burning urge to speak. I wanted to share with him all I knew about the journey of the soul. Understanding the Jewish view of the afterlife would help him deal with his father and his past, but I knew the time for sharing this ancient wisdom wasn't right yet.

Every time I was tempted to speak, I thought of Aaron, the High Priest of the Bible, who tragically lost his two eldest sons on the opening day of the Tabernacle. Moses, Aaron's younger brother, tried to comfort him by explaining the philosophical reason for the tragedy. But Aaron remained silent. By *not* stating that Aaron was comforted by his brother's rationale, and instead making mention of Aaron's choice to remain quiet, the biblical narrative subtly suggests that silence is the wiser approach to dealing with tragedy and death. So I kept quiet, holding Jerry in a long embrace.

I had a vivid flashback of Jerry as a young man coming to synagogue when Morris sponsored the Kiddush luncheon in honor of his birthday, when the father and son were business partners. Morris's face was beaming with pride as Jerry got up to say a few words in honor of his dad. Morris embraced him. It was a picture of a man holding on tightly to a treasure he didn't ever want to part with.

When Jerry was growing up, Morris told me how Jerry was the epicenter of his life, his one and only son. After Morris survived the war, he moved to Ottawa where he eventually reconnected with Anna, an old friend from the *shtetl* and a fellow Holocaust survivor. They married, and gave birth to a beautiful boy they named Jerry, after Moshe's father, Yerachmiel, who perished in Auschwitz. They fondly called Jerry their "Kaddishel," a Yiddish term traditionally used by Jews for an only son in anticipation that, upon his parents' deaths, he would recite Kaddish, the memorial prayer for the dead.

Over the years, Morris reminded me of this expectation that they had of Jerry. Only a few days before he died, Morris made me promise, among other things, that I would convince Jerry to say the Kaddish prayer. Knowing Jerry, it seemed like an impossible task. He had drifted far away from his roots and was unapologetic about his lack of faith.

Holding Jerry now, the promise hovered in my thoughts. Reason told me it was not the time to remind him of his father's Kaddish wish now, even though his animosity toward me was temporarily lifted. I hoped this thaw between us would last long enough for me to honor Morris's Kaddish wish.

As Jerry calmed down, I released the embrace. To my surprise, Jerry began to speak: "Thanks for the hug. I just can't believe it's over, and I never made up with him. I feel like my father's up there looking down with anger at me, his wayward son. But honestly, what could I have done differently? Anyway, game over, as they say."

His hopelessness was jarring and I blurted out more than I meant to. "Jerry," I said. "Do you sincerely believe that a whole lifetime of precious memories are just buried in the ground? There's more to a person than just the temporary body, there's an everlasting soul. There is a way for you to reconnect with your father."

"A soul?" Jerry said, pulling away from me. "There you go again with your old-fashioned superstition."

I had spoken out of turn, caught up in thoughts of Morris. I was stuck now. I had learned that it was better not to backtrack and apologize for my religious jargon. I had to own my role as rabbi. "I know it sounds like ghosts and magic, but there is a unique soul in each of us."

"How can you expect me to believe in G–d after what I saw my believing father go through in the hospital, during his last hellish days on earth?" Jerry asked softly. I nodded. His father had experienced the darkest days of humanity, survived, and then battled cancer.

The sound of cars pulling into the driveway floated into the room where we were standing. Jerry's wife came to announce that supper was ready. As I patted his arm, Jerry said, to my surprise, "To be continued, Rabbi."

I nodded as Jerry looked me in the eyes and showed me to the door.

The Backstory

On the car ride back to my home, all I could think about was Morris and Jerry.

> Morris and his wife Anna had provided Jerry with all of his needs and wants. He was their number one priority and focus. Notwithstanding Morris's hectic work schedule, he always made it his business to spend quality time with his Kaddishel. The two of them would never miss going out to the hockey game together once a week, and, of course, to Morris's favorite place—the synagogue, where he loved sitting side by side with his son on the Sabbath to pray.

But those were the days when Jerry was close to his father, before Jerry became a business superstar and wealthy entrepreneur; and before he had carved out his own path in life.

Their departing paths could be traced back to right after Jerry's bar mitzvah, when he began his rebellious teenage years. Gradually, he slipped out of the religious mold, like many of his peers.

Morris was obviously very upset about the change of direction in Jerry's life, especially in light of his own personal dedication to Judaism. Yet, to his credit, Morris tried very hard to maintain a strong bond with his son, despite their growing differences in spiritual matters.

But Jerry didn't make it easy. He joined the popular hippie movement of the 'sixties, grew his hair long, and spoke of peace and love. He went to Woodstock and became a part of the new world of flower children that rejected everything their parents stood for. At one point, he flirted with drugs, overdosing on cocaine.

Anna and Morris were devastated when they nearly lost Jerry. The social revolution of the sixties had stolen their warm relationship with their only son, who seemed to be on a path of reckless destruction. But then, a few years later, like many of his peers, Jerry got over the hype and found his way back to the conservative family values he was raised on. He joined his father's business and slowly climbed the corporate ladder. From warehouse stocker, Jerry grew into a pragmatic businessman. They seemed a perfect working match for each other. And once he had married and had a child, Jerry was, in every way, his father's son....

Except in matters of religion or politics, of course. Jerry could never understand how a survivor of the Holocaust could make amends with G–d; it really bothered him. Especially difficult for Jerry was Morris's commitment to supporting Jewish institutions through generous financial contributions. Jerry feared these donations politicized the business, and he felt that it would be better for the business if the company focused on reinvesting the profits into the company rather than donating to sectarian causes.

Meanwhile, those of us on the receiving end of Morris's generosity were dumbfounded by his commitment to his faith. Religious rejection was a common reaction to the Holocaust. How G–d could allow such horrors—six million Jews killed because of one man's charismatic spreading of hatred—did not make sense. There was no explanation that could justify sick, sadistic medical experiments on innocent children. Yet Morris unfailingly showed up to synagogue smiling, handing out candy. His wife, Anna, seemed more reticent to get involved with the community, but she was a reserved and elegant woman who subtly supported our synagogue's sisterhood.

Morris had hoped that Jerry would find solace in traditional Judaism. Yet who knows what ghosts haunted Jerry's parents in the privacy of their home. Is that what fueled Jerry's teenage rebellion? Whatever it was that had caused Jerry to feel animosity toward Judaism, his strong negative feelings amplified as Jerry got older, and his children also drifted away from their heritage.

Despite these differences, Morris never interfered with Jerry's personal or religious life, and a mutual respect between father and son usually prevailed. But, one epic episode changed that status quo forever.

It all started with an innocuous family trip to Europe. You see, Jerry had a secret religion—sports. For as long as I knew him, he ate and breathed sports. Two years prior to the passing of Morris, during the summer, Jerry took his family to Europe to see the Olympics. Unfortunately, Morris's older sister— Jerry's aunt, who had moved to Montreal before the war, the only other surviving relative of the family—passed away at that time. Morris obviously expected Jerry to return home for the funeral, but Jerry refused. Jerry felt that his attendance at her funeral would not bring his aunt back to life and that the Olympic Games were too compelling to miss.

Morris was deeply hurt by Jerry's absence at the funeral. He expected better. While he had never commented on or tried to influence Jerry's religious path, Morris valued family over everything. Not showing up to the funeral or shivah week was a betrayal of that sacred family bond. I had never seen Morris so unsettled, and I worried for his health. "Jerry should worry," he told me, when I expressed my concern. Nevertheless, Jerry returned from his trip tanned and content. He seemed to make peace with Morris, and the two continued their successful partnership.

Yet six months later, a high-profit billion-dollar business deal came up with a company that had sympathized with the Nazis in World War II.

Jerry was thrilled their family firm had grown so much as to be recognized and sought after by an international brand name. Morris was disgusted that Jerry would even consider partnering with that firm because of their Nazi past.

"What has happened to my son?" Morris lamented after services one morning. He has no respect for the past and for the suffering of our people. Where did I go wrong?"

By the end of that bleak year, father and son stopped speaking to each other. Jerry took his fortune and started his own company, using ads and lingo Morris never would have approved. Anna sent Jerry's child and grandchild birthday gifts and was still allowed entry into Jerry's narrowing world. But not Morris. Neither father nor son would budge.

Morris spoke to me many times about this altercation with Jerry and their subsequent rift. It hurt him tremendously, and while he spoke many times about possible reconciliation, it never materialized. You know what they say, "Too little, too late"? They both were too entrenched in their positions and both were equally stubborn.

As I pulled into my driveway, my boys — the grandkids — ran to greet me. I hugged each one of them tight, hoping we would stay close forever, never allowing a rift to form between us.

My wife, Chana, stood in the brightly lit doorway, smiling as we neared. The aroma of a delicious supper welcomed me. I was so glad to be home. The boys seemed to sense that I needed some downtime and went off to play. My wife sat next to me as I sipped the soup she offered.

"How is Jerry holding up?" she asked gently. She knew I had been apprehensive about the *shivah* call, feeling stuck between my promise to Morris and Jerry's wish to avoid rabbis and synagogues, especially mine, forever.

"Worse than I expected," I answered honestly. "He seems different somehow—sensitive and vulnerable."

Chana nodded. "It's so painful to lose a parent. A huge loss."

"Yes. It's just..." I hesitated, wondering how to explain Jerry's sudden warmth to me, his openness. "He was really shaken up and seemed like he wanted to talk to me about his father."

"His wife, Lisa, called while you were driving home and said she wanted to make sure you knew about the memorial breakfast tomorrow," Chana added. "Jerry is really reaching out. And, believe it or not," she paused, "she told me that while he was not planning on observing the whole week of the shivah he wants to say the Kaddish memorial prayer at the memorial breakfast."

"Wow, that's great news," I answered, remembering my promise to Morris just before he died. "But I wonder what the catch is. He was so angry before the funeral...so convinced that I was after his father's fortune. Why the sudden change?"

"Well, maybe he could sense your sincerity and your own grief at the cemetery. Or maybe, he just needs support," Chana tried.

I sighed. "Supper is delicious," I said, leaning back in my chair. "I don't know. We are going to have to stop the planned construction on the new facility without Morris's pledged contribution. Not just the money. He gave me confidence, built me up since we arrived here. He was like a father to me, Chana."

"G–d will find a way to work out the money, whether Jerry distributes it from Morris's estate or not," Chana said calmly. "Things have been tight, but the money works out somehow, every time."

I shook my head. The stakes were high for a new building for the synagogue. A new rabbi had taken over a large congregation in the next township over. He was young, dynamic, and a successful fundraiser. His programming tapped into the *zeitgeist*, and young professionals seemed drawn to this charismatic new rabbi in town. My aim was to serve my congregation, the community. I had no aim to become a guru or advisor to the stars. Yet it was difficult to feel overshadowed by the hip marketing of the Kabbalah workshops and meditation groups. I had to remind myself that I wasn't selling Judaism. I was here to support my community.

The challenge was supporting my family at the same time. After years of growing, my congregation was slowly downsizing. Many of the younger set had moved to Montreal or Toronto to get married, and those who stayed were not interested in expanding our synagogue. They had their friends, cliques, interests, and causes. When I tried starting a new class, the old crew shot me down, and didn't approve funds for flyers and ads to publicize the event. I was starting to feel burned-out and dejected, ready for early retirement at 52. Jerry was my same age and seemed to be hitting his stride, at least in his business life. Why was I struggling?

"I know you're discouraged," Chana added. "But you can't carry out Morris's wishes to connect with Jerry if your primary concern is financial. The money will work out. Just do your job."

"You make it sound easy, Chana," I answered. "But it's not. Between Rabbi Cohen going after the younger crowd, and…"

"I know," Chana interrupted. "But you must trust G–d. We are going to be OK. The synagogue will grow again."

I stood up and cleared my plate. The warmth in our home soothed me. Chana turned on music as she swept up, and she prepared the table for the next day as a batch of her legendary chocolate cookies were baking in the oven. I looked out the kitchen window, staring at the old tree we had planted years ago. It was mature now, like our children who had grown up playing in its strong branches, but had now moved on to the next stage in life.

"I sure hope so," I said, breaking the comfortable silence.

Chana smiled. Then the phone rang. It was our youngest son, Mendy, who was studying in New York. He was calling me for our weekly Torah learning session. After a quick check-in, Chana passed the phone to me. I walked to my study, trying to push aside thoughts of failure and jagged memories of Morris, as my son began reading the holy text.

"Are you there, Dad?" Mendy asked gently. He could sense that I was out of sorts.

"Yes, I'm following along," I reassured him. "Just a little worn out. I don't know if Mommy told you, but Morris passed away."

"Mommy told me yesterday," Mendy said. "I'm devastated, Dad. I can't even imagine how you're feeling. And you had to get up and give the eulogy, and also navigated the funeral with Jerry."

"Just doing my job," I said, but it wasn't enough. Nothing could really capture the loss I felt. Morris had been there for me every event, every holiday. Practically every dollar I ever raised and every sermon I gave had been inspired, approved, and supported by Morris. He was my core pillar. And yet, I had no formal way to mourn my mentor and friend. No *shivah*. As the rabbi, it was my job to put my emotions aside and help Morris's family grieve the loss of their patriarch and fierce protector.

Mendy and I finally settled into our routine of Torah learning. I appreciated Mendy's insights, feeling proud of his continued interest in our shared community congregants, and in our culture, religion, and identity. While life was full of struggles for me and my grown children, I felt grateful to connect with them: grateful that, while I could not provide much financial support, the way many business moguls could, I was able to bond with my son over the ancient words of the Torah that has guided Jewish practice and belief until today.

I turned off the kitchen lights and snuck one of Chana's still-warm cookies before climbing the stairs to bed. What a tiring and emotional day. And now I had to show up at Jerry's for breakfast. I wanted to think positively about the invitation, but I was a little apprehensive.

The Breakfast

The breakfast had already started by the time I showed up five minutes late. Silver-haired men in business suits nodded courteously as I passed and took my seat near Jerry's family at the front of the room. Jerry shot me a look for my tardiness. I hadn't known I was an important guest at this memorial breakfast, especially since I had only been invited the night before.

"Now that the rabbi's here, we can finally begin," Jerry said to the crowded room. A caterer had set up tables around Jerry's living and dining areas, with sumptuous buffets filled with breakfast food. Waiters cleared and served. Everyone was checking their cell phones. My thoughts were racing as it dawned on me that Jerry expected me to speak and lead him in the Kaddish prayer.

My whirlwind of a morning flashed before me. A leak in the synagogue had caused a ruckus and delayed the morning services, leading to complaints and a frantic call to the plumber. Now I was here, standing in front of Ottawa's most prominent businessmen and still mentally switching gears.

I had once hoped to capture the attention of the city's Jewish dealmakers to build interest in our synagogue. But that was decades ago. Meanwhile, here I was with the access and opportunity to connect with these secular Jewish leaders in our community, and I was completely unprepared.

Jerry leaned close to me and whispered, "Rabbi Goldstein, I'd like you to give my friends some insight about who my father was, since you knew him so well and he appreciated you so dearly. And can you please explain the meaning of this ancient prayer that I'm about to recite. I know it's supposed to help my father's soul, but I don't know if I even believe in it."

My heart was in my throat as I approached the podium. What on earth could I say that would satisfy Jerry, inspire the crowd, and honor Morris?

"When I talk about the soul of Morris, I'm not speaking about ghosts or spirits. I'm speaking about a real part of us. Yes, the soul may be spiritual, but it is still a real, inseparable part of who we are. While we may interact and communicate mostly with the physical parts of our being, I'm sure that you will all agree that there is another more elusive dimension to each one of us. There is obviously a part of us that loves and fears, that thinks and desires, that's happy and sad. At times, it is creative, and at times, destructive. It makes choices and has pleasure. It takes pride in our children and their successes. It is the very essence of what we consider life itself."

"Nonsense rabbi, it's the brain that does all of that!" Jerry called out. I heard a loud murmur in the crowd. People were shaking their heads. The negativity was palpable.

After waiting for the audience to quiet down, I continued. "Do you really think that your legend of a father was merely a physical body and brain? Can it be that such a great man ceases to exist? The soul is who we *really* are; it is our *true* identity. It works behind the scenes, manipulating and utilizing our brain as it chooses, like a mouse on a computer screen. And then, when we die, even though the brain disintegrates with the rest of the body, our soul remains alive, forever. Your father's soul is alive, Jerry..."

The audience clapped feebly as I stepped away from the microphone.

I returned to my seat, dejected and barely able to make eye contact with my tablemates. I felt so bad for being confrontational with Jerry. It was my bad mood, I thought. I wished I could sneak out, but every time I moved my chair, another speaker began recounting his memories of Morris.

Finally, the breakfast was over, Kaddish was said and I headed toward the door. I was surprised to feel a tap on my shoulder, holding me back.

It was Jerry. "Rabbi, I hear in your voice how much you miss my father. It may feel right that my father lives on, but it's just wishful thinking."

"Listen, I know it's hard to believe, Jerry, but I have studied this stuff. Think about your father's noble qualities, his good nature, his kindness. Where do you think all of that went? And what about his outstanding piety and spirituality? You know very well how he loved coming to synagogue every day to pray. It was an absolute pleasure watching him. After years of being a rabbi, one can sense when prayers are genuine or not. Morris was an unusually serious congregant. When he prayed, you could see a person engaged in a personal conversation with G–d. The occasional tear running down his cheeks told the story of a man opening up his wounds before his maker.

Jerry unfolded his arms, nodding his head as I share my memories of Morris. I continued sharing what Morris had done for me, unable to stop what I had started:

"Whenever doubts would creep into my own mind about my faith, I would find inspiration in your father, especially in the way he stayed strong despite what he had lived through. I can't imagine how such unparalleled piety and inspiration would just disappear permanently. I can't even begin to think about how much I owe your father. Everyone knew that he was the financial pillar of our community synagogue…" I hesitated awkwardly.

Our small synagogue, Anshei Emeth, was traditional Orthodox and, like many others, struggled financially. Morris was our go-to man. Not only did he help build our little synagogue in the early days, he continued to offer financial support to bail us out in the recent tough times as well. In fact, he had promised me recently that he would leave an endowment fund in his will to help build a magnificent new synagogue.

But, now, I seriously doubted whether Jerry would honor his father's pledges. Our synagogue could really use the help. We had been struggling mightily to stay afloat since the younger, hipper rabbi had opened a center nearby. I'd been hoping that a new building would turn things around for us. Without Morris's moral and financial support, I wasn't sure what would happen. But I'd be there for Jerry, no matter what. I owed it to Morris. Plus, I had never become a community rabbi for the money. Yet the truth was, if things didn't turn around, my congregation might not make it much longer.

I saw Jerry flinch at the mention of his father's financial support of my synagogue. He was a sharp man. "I thought we'd get to the money eventually, but not this quick," Jerry muttered under his breath.

I couldn't take back what I'd said, so I went back to Morris, the only connection Jerry and I had. "Jerry, these amazing traits of your father don't just disappear. There is a part of each one of us that lasts forever, and that's the soul," I told him. I wished he could understand how his soul—how especially his father's soul —was knit into the fabric of the Jewish people forever.

"Again, Rabbi, I would love it to be true, but I just don't believe in this stuff. What makes you so sure that there's a soul, aside from your religious doctrine and faith?"

I felt Jerry getting edgy. I felt guilty that he was walking me to the door instead of speaking with his friends and family at the buffet. I felt I owed him something after bringing up so much of the past.

"Jerry, how do you view life? I am interested to know what you believe it is that animates the body."

"You're asking me what I think makes us alive, Rabbi? Frankly, the heartbeat, brain waves, and oxygen sustain the body and energize it," he responded.

"Yes, of course," I replied. "The physical body uses oxygen, the heart pumps blood. But the physical body gradually deteriorates when the "warranty" on its parts expires, but the life force that animates it remains intact. Death for the soul always seems to be abrupt, not gradual," I continued, hoping to parse out this spiritual force in all living things.

"But Rabbi, don't we sometimes see that when a person is near death, their enthusiasm for life does wane and their energy levels *do* go down as well?"

"Yes. Even though we may say that someone looks 'half dead,' really, there is no such thing. It is the *body* failing. Yet, for the soul, death is a transitional split second and not a process," I added.

I heard the hum of voices from the breakfast coming nearer to the entrance where I stood with Jerry. This was an intense conversation to be having standing up, with so many other people present. I worried that I had taxed the new mourner in my efforts to alleviate his raw pain.

I leaned in close to Jerry, and suddenly I felt a deep need to share the last image I had of Morris, the holy survivor from Auschwitz who had entrusted me to care for his son's soul.

"I was there when your father died, Jerry. And I clearly saw that sparkle in your father's eyes until his very last breath. Even as your father's body was clearly failing him, his soul remained strong: courageous and fully intact. His soul was and still is an unbridled energy from another infinite space."

"I hear your point, but I'm not convinced," Jerry said, as he reached toward the door, releasing both of us from this intense exchange. "Perhaps that's because I wasn't there in my father's last moments."

It was just one day after the funeral and he was emotionally raw. So was I. He patted my back, as the throng of important breakfast people headed for the door. I could see that Jerry was very tired. I said a quick goodbye, hoping that I had offered a measure of comfort to Jerry—hoping, as well, that I'd planted a seed for further thought.

The Birthday

The next occasion to talk came faster than I'd expected. Two weeks later, Jerry was throwing a birthday party for his young granddaughter, Jordana. Generally, parties during the first year of mourning, and particularly the first thirty days, are not in keeping with Jewish tradition. But Jerry had no intention of ruining his granddaughter's birthday because of his personal loss. It was going to be a "Jerry-style" party, no holds barred.

Meanwhile, I was exhausted and frustrated. There was another leak now in the synagogue roof, right near the ark. I had heard that the new shul of my competition was growing and had gotten the attention of some of the big business leaders at Jerry's *shivah*-week breakfast, where my ill-received speech had ruffled the crowd. I felt old and worn out, not in the mood for a bois-terous birthday party.

"You're doing this for Morris," my wife reminded me as I walked out the door.

There was traffic on the way, and I took the opportunity to reconnect with what I could offer Jerry, which was friendship, support, and kindness. That's all I had. As I walked in through the front door of the beautiful mansion, I was awed by the opulence. Rushing to the breakfast and at the bereavement call, I had overlooked the magnificent furnishings—the massive chandeliers, the oversized furniture accented with gold and silver, the original oil paintings signed by master painters—and I wondered whether Jerry would really be at all interested in any spiritual guidance.

Over the years in my work as a Rabbi, I've found that too much wealth can dull a person's spiritual appetite. No longer uncertain about material survival, people seemed to disconnect from seeking help from an invisible divine force. There were exceptions of course, like Morris, who maintained strong values in spite of their prosperity. For my wife and me, observing this pattern emphasized the importance of raising our children in a healthy, balanced environment with not too much, and not too little. Obviously I did not have the same test of wealth that Jerry encountered, yet I saw that money did not guarantee happiness, or close relationships.

As I continued walking through Jerry's elegant house, it was difficult not to compare our small, well-kept home with this grand mansion. Finally, I reached the backyard where the birthday party was unfolding by the pool. In contrast to the broken Jerry I saw at the funeral, I beheld a handsome executive standing with his picture-perfect wife and daughter. His daughter looked to be pregnant with another child, but she carried herself with extreme elegance. Three-year old granddaughter Jordana was filled with excitement as she opened beautifully wrapped gifts and ate purple candy. Still, Jerry was the central attraction, with everyone dying to catch his attention and make some conversation with this powerful businessman.

When he spotted me from the corner of his eye, Jerry called me over. I was surprised when he sheepishly started to apologize for celebrating a birthday party so close to his father's funeral. I was never sure how familiar Jerry was with Jewish tradition and practice—how much he remembered from his childhood.

"I know that my father would never have approved of this party so quickly after the funeral," Jerry said strongly. It wasn't an apology, and I certainly wasn't demanding an explanation. "But, hey, Dad and I never saw eye-to-eye on religious matters, especially since our big fallout. I'm sure you know about that."

Boy, was I caught off guard. I wasn't expecting Jerry to bring up the fight with his father at a kids' party. Perhaps he was testing our fragile connection, unraveling the awkward triangle between Morris, Jerry, and me. I also wondered: *What kept drawing Jerry to me, and me to Jerry?*

Three-year-old Jordana and her toddling friends were occupied with the face painter and the balloon artist. Jerry's wife Lisa and his daughter snapped pictures of the adorable antics.

Jerry continued talking amid delighted squeals of laughter. "As you know, I disagreed with my father on religious matters. Yet I still consider myself a spiritual person. Our chat about the soul the other day really struck something in me. I'd love to ask you some more questions."

"Go for it, Jerry," I replied, still hesitant. I glanced at the happy children, and marveled at the contrast. Jerry was smiling on the outside, and yet his thoughts were with his father.

"The existence of a soul resonates with me on an emotional level. Yet I'm still not clear about how you can be so sure that it exists. We may feel it intuitively, but how can we guarantee that it's not the physical brain calling the shots?" Jerry ventured.

I paused, thinking how best to present the inner workings of an invisible spiritual force. "True, the brain is a highly wondrous, versatile, and comprehensive instrument that controls the workings of the body. Yet there are essential experiences that cannot be traced back to the brain," I said.

Jerry nodded expectantly.

"Yes, we know science has discovered many locations in the brain that control and monitor mostly everything. They have even been successful in locating parts of the brain in which some of the deepest human emotions are experienced, like pain and pleasure," I tried. "But as much as they have tried, they can't seem to place their finger on the love center. Love is generally considered by scientists as a *terra incognita*, an unknown land. How can something as essential as love have no home address?" The children splashed in the pool. The wives chatted breezily as they kept an eye on their offspring.

"Take, for example, your deep love for Jordana," I pointed to the birthday girl. "Is that feeling emanating from your brain or from somewhere deeper? Perhaps it comes from your essence: a place that existed before you were born and will continue after you die?"

Jerry turned to look at the party. His focus stayed on Jordana, as she played with her friends.

"And how about your dear wife, Lisa?"

"What do you mean, Rabbi?" Jerry said, turning his attention back to me.

"Well, this is a little personal, but why are you attracted to her? How do you explain the attraction? Why are we strongly attracted to some people, to the point that we may even want to marry them? Isn't it strange that some people may find another person attractive while others are repulsed by the very same person? There is something that makes two people gravitate toward each other with a powerful force. This connection obviously transcends the logical brain. I'd argue that it emanates from a deep space in the soul." I continued.

Jerry rapped his fingers on the table where we sat. He looked briefly toward Lisa, but I couldn't tell what he was thinking. He didn't elaborate on his love for his wife. And I didn't push him to, either. I quickly switched topics.

"OK, let's take it from a business perspective," I tried.

"What's that, Rabbi?" Jerry tuned back in, looking relieved.

I'd found common ground.

Well, Jerry, everyone knows that you run a highly successful business, driven by creativity and innovation. Of course, there are many great ideas formulated by analytical thinking and logical resonance," I said, wiping my brow. The sun was brighter now, and the air felt humid.

"Yes," Jerry answered, signaling for me to continue.

"But then there are the ideas that just come out of the blue. They just show up! They appear like a lightning bolt or like that figurative light bulb over our heads. The 'Aha!' moment emanates from the soul," I said.

Jerry looked engaged. "Yes, I call those money moments, Rabbi. They almost always pay off."

"So in my experience, these ideas don't arrive when we're in control, but when we're relaxing, taking a shower or a walk. Paul McCartney first wrote down his famous song *Yesterday* on the back of a brown envelope, and the first verse of *Bridge Over Troubled Water* came to Paul Simon while he gazed out a window at the East River in Manhattan," I shared, hoping to keep my growing connection with Jerry.

"Hey, Rabbi, how do you know about the Beatles and Simon and Garfunkel? Isn't that forbidden territory for a guy like you?" Jerry asked in surprise.

I laughed. "Gotta keep up with my congregation, Jerry."

"Well, you could probably get a little more current," he added with a chuckle.

I smiled. There was a part of me that was stuck in the old days, unsure of how to keep up with the current trends. I resented my struggle, since I had prided myself on keeping pace and even trailblazing with events, technology, and creative ways to connect with my community. Yet, Jerry was right.

"Science says that these ideas emerge from the subconscious, but where is that exactly? This brain behind the brain is where the real person lies, and it's called the soul," I told him, reaching over to pat his shoulder. I felt like we were talking in circles.

He shook his head, not quite ready to buy into my reasoning.

"Or how about your sense of fairness in business? I know, Jerry, that you have a stellar reputation regarding the way you treat your employees and clients. Where does that come from? It's what we call our inner moral compass. There is something inside of us that practically compels us to be fair and just. There is nothing in the brain to support that." I continued relentlessly, hoping to find a way he could connect to the concept of a soul.

"Okay, I hear what you're saying," countered Jerry. "Thanks for all the unnecessary compliments, but how do you expect me to believe in a soul that I can't even see? This is, after all, the twenty-first century, and it doesn't sound very scientific to me to believe in things that we can't actually touch or feel!"

"Yes, I agree. Science is very important. It helps us deal with observable phenomena. But let's be honest: Not everything in this world is visible. Failing to see something is no proof that it doesn't exist. There are, in fact, all sorts of invisible phenomena moving all around us on a constant basis, and yet no one would ever deny their existence. There are airwaves and sound waves, wireless communication and X-rays, bacteria and viruses, and the list goes on and on. Sometimes I wonder how there is any room left in this world for us humans when there is such a massive, invisible world sharing the same space," I answered, as a pink balloon floated up to the sky.

I had chosen the example of wireless communication because that's where Jerry made his fortune. He sat back in his chair, thinking…processing. I thought about how we both had ended up together at a lavish pool party, discussing the divine soul.

After Jerry got married and had three children of his own,
like most of his peers, he moved out to suburbia, settled down,

raised a family and got busy coaching his kids at hockey. All the idealism and chaos of his youth were replaced with a love of money and material wealth.

With a little help from his father, Jerry moved quickly up the ladder in Morris's business and Jerry soon became CEO. But that's not where it ended for Jerry. Besides the fortune he managed for his father, he made a greater fortune on his own.

From a very young age, Jerry loved computers; he could be called a computer geek. One day, while playing with his computer, he developed a revolutionary communication app that would change the way people do business everywhere. Jerry successfully marketed this app and never looked back. He became one of the most successful entrepreneurs in all of Canada because of his innovative mind and competitive, entrepreneurial spirit.

A minute had passed and Jerry was still quiet. So I filled the silence with another story that came to mind.

There was a freshman in college, starting his first day of classes who brought this powerful point home to his professor.

His teacher was clearly an atheist and started the day by saying the following: "Students, is there anyone here who can see G–d? If so, raise your hand. If there is anyone here who can hear G–d, please raise your hand. If there is anyone who can smell G–d, raise your hand." After a short pause, with no response from the students, the professor concluded, "Since no one can see, smell, or hear G–d, this must prove conclusively that there is no G–d."

A student then raised his hand and asked to address the class. The student approached the class and asked, "Students, can anyone here see the professor's brain? Can anyone hear the professor's brain? Can anyone smell the professor's brain?"

After a short pause, he concluded, "Since no one can see, hear or smell the professor's brain, this proves conclusively that he has no brain!"

"You see, simply not seeing a soul is no proof it doesn't exist! We don't see the soul because it's invisible, and that's it," I explained.

"But come on, Rabbi," insisted Jerry. "I saw the other day with my own eyes how they buried my father six feet beneath the ground. There is no doubt in my mind that my father is dead and finished. How can you tell me otherwise?"

"What precisely did you see being buried? Your father's body, not his soul. Unlike his body, his beautiful soul continues to live on eternally," I explained.

Jerry looked frustrated. But I wasn't going to give up on this.

"You see, although 'created in the image of G–d,' the body is just a sophisticated, temporary piece of machinery that facilitates the soul in this world. The body is the soul's 'hands and feet,' and allows the soul to express itself in a meaningful manner during its short stay in this world."

"OK," Jerry said. "Keep going on this."

"Body and soul are an inseparable team and they spend a lifetime helping each other, but their end is very different. While the body returns to the universe's ecological system— 'Dust to dust,' as we say in our prayers—the soul returns to its own source, in the heavens above. The soul has its own unique 'spiritual' ecological system," I explained.

"But, Rabbi, how can any part of this universe, where everything else dies, go on living forever? Logic dictates that even the soul should play by the same rules of this universe and eventually expire. Why should the soul be an exception?" Jerry asked, suddenly more engaged.

"Not everything in this universe was made to be subject to death," I responded.

We were interrupted by the precocious birthday girl. She dragged her grandfather by his leg, with a little mischievous smile on her face while holding onto an unblown balloon in her hand. Her grandfather immediately understood what was expected of him.

36

"Grandpa, can you blow up this birthday balloon for me?" Jordana asked sweetly.

"Jordana, my dear, you know how much Grandpa hates blowing balloons, but for you, my little angel, give me that balloon, and I will gladly blow it for you!"

Jerry immediately began the arduous task of filling the balloon with air.

"Jerry, do you by any chance happen to know who the first one in the world was to ever blow up a balloon?"

Jerry shrugged his shoulders while struggling to fill the balloon with all the air he had saved in the recesses of his lungs.

"It was none other than G–d himself, the Creator of Heaven and earth. The Bible tells us that G–d infused in Adam a soul of life, described as the 'breath of G–d.' The verse says, 'And G–d blew into his nostrils a breath of life.' Quite an extensive and wondrous 'balloon'—those lungs of the original man, eh?" I said as Jerry took a quick break from the balloon.

"Obviously this anthropomorphic description of blowing was not meant to be taken literally as is the case with much of the imagery of the Bible. Blowing a breath into this newly-created man was meant as some kind of metaphor to teach us a lesson. So tell me, why would the Bible choose the metaphor of *breath* to describe this infusion of a soul into Adam? Why not just simply say 'and He graciously presented Adam a soul'?" I added.

"Got me there Rabbi! Good question. Never thought of it!" said Jerry. Jordana waited expectantly for her grandfather to finish filling the bright pink balloon.

"This original description must have been chosen by the author of the world's best-seller, with great deliberation, to give us some deeper insight into the soul," I said, smiling. Jerry was blowing into the balloon again.

"You have a lot to say, Rabbi," Jordana piped in. I chuckled.

"This metaphor teaches us that, unlike the body, the soul is an eternal piece of G–d and, therefore, life should be revered and never squandered," I said as Jerry's balloon grew fuller.

"Just like the human breath that originates from the deepest cavities of man, from the "aching insides" you are feeling right now as you exhale your breath into a balloon, the soul too, originates from the deepest and most intimate cavities of the Divine," I added.

I was watching Jerry struggling to blow into his granddaughter's balloon. It was a really big one, and I imagined how his chest must have really been aching by now. But despite the pain, Jerry looked really proud of his little creation that he had fashioned for his precious Jordana.

Jordana took her balloon happily, and raced back to her friends at her party.

"So there you have it Jerry. The soul's source is the breath of G–d, and although it shares the same space in this world with a mortal body, the soul itself is of a completely different genre. It is a divine piece that is never subjected to the limitations of this world and it never dies." I was done, and so was Jerry. I saw the women preparing the cake moment of the party, and I imagined that Jerry wanted to join in the festivities again.

Instead, he prodded me on the balloon example.

"I hear your point, Rabbi but I still don't get it. If I may challenge your balloon metaphor, a balloon — as you can see — is just a cheap measly piece of rubber, whereas the human body is, like the soul, a glorious creation 'made in "the image of G–d'" as you said? So if the soul remains indestructible because of its divine origin, shouldn't the body share some of that same destiny?"

"Jerry, that's a great question. The body was created in the *image* of G–d, while the soul is actually a *piece* of G–d."

Jerry looked puzzled. "Now you're parsing words. It's all the same thing."

"When a great artist, like Picasso or Van Gogh, paints a beautiful and colorful painting, we name the painting after the artist who painted it. We call it affectionately a *Picasso* or a *Van Gogh*! But alas, are they really Picassos and Van Goghs? They may have been fashioned by the master artists, but they surely aren't Van Gogh or Picasso. Try pinching the painting and see if they shout! We call them *Van Gogh* and *Picasso* only because the paintings reflect the particular genius and unique talents of the artists! In truth, however, we are looking at nothing more than a painting on canvas—that's all."

Jerry looked amused at my example. He had a small smile on his face, and I felt I was entertaining him, at least.

"The human body is G–d's excellent painting. Every limb and every blood vessel—every single cell—shouts out the absolute unfathomable genius of G–d. No scientist, biologist, or doctor can replicate even a single cell of the human body from scratch. The more we learn about the body, the more we are simply blown away by its absolute genius. We give one look at the body and proclaim, 'Wow, that's a *Van G–d*,'" I said.

Jerry laughed, tossing his head of thick silver hair back in a howl of laughter. "You are a funny man, Rabbi."

"Yet, despite its awesomeness, the human body is only a mere 'image' of its Creator. It is not an actual *piece* of the Creator. The soul, on the other hand, Jerry, is not just an image, it is a piece of the Divine. It is the breath of G–d. And because it is a *piece* of the Divine, it is indestructible and lives on forever."

"You are passionate about this topic, Rabbi," Jerry said. "That's for sure."

Jordana ran to fetch us for cake and the main party activity. "Grandpa! Come with me. Let's go make a kite and fly it together!"

I watched as Jordana *shlepped* Jerry to the kite-flying birthday activity area, where all the guests were already busy creating their own unique personalized kites in preparation for flying them in the park behind Jerry's mansion. Jerry joined Jordana in making the kite and then in trying to fly it.

"Come on, Rabbi! Come and fly the kites with us," Jerry urged.

As Jordana began flying her birthday kite way up in the sky, a low drifting cloud encircled the kite and hid it from view. It almost looked like the kite was gone. A pedestrian passing by, an older-looking gentleman, tried to make some conversation with spunky Jordana and asked her what she was doing with that string in her hand.

"I'm flying my kite," she responded.

The man looked up and, seeing only the cloud in an otherwise clear sky, said, "I don't see any kite up there anywhere. You must be kidding me!"

"No, sir," the little girl replied, "I don't see it either, but I know it's up there.

"But how do you know for sure?" asked the man. If you don't see it, perhaps it's gone by now?" the man pushed.

"Every once in a while there's a pull on my string that lets me know that it's still there." Jordana explained confidently.

Jerry piped in, "You don't need to see the soul to know that it exists. If every once in a while there's a tug on the string you can be certain it exists. Isn't that right, Rabbi?" He winked at me, as his kite flew higher.

"That's right, Jerry. You're catching on to this very well!" I was very impressed with Jerry's observation. "And let's call this 'tug' of the soul that we are speaking about 'faith.' We all experience this from time to time—an inexplicable strong feeling of faith that tugs us deep inside. This enigmatic feeling arrives, without ever warning us and at the strangest of times. Sometimes it comes during moments of tragedy and sometimes during moments of joy, but it is always that same profound feeling of being drawn to something greater than ourselves." I added.

"Oh, Rabbi: How is it that you turn everything you see into a lesson? Can't you just live and have some fun with us?"

"There is so much we can learn from everything we see!" I replied, taking the hint to back off the heavy conversation.

"Rabbi," said Jerry, trying to change the subject, "Talking about human weakness, how about joining me as we honor the birthday girl by indulging in some decadent birthday cake? After all, this is her party and not a philosophy class!" Jerry then grabbed me by the arm and *shlepped* me back to the poolside to witness a cake like I'd never seen before! This birthday cake was made of seven levels of breathtaking artistic detail.

Jordana was beaming ear to ear and was standing in front of the cake.

"*Nu*, Jordana?" said a proud Jerry. "Before we eat the exquisite cake, make a wish in honor of your birthday and blow out the candles."

Jordana, who had a funny sense of humor for a kid her age, closed her eyes tight and said:

"I wish Grandpa would stop talking already so that I could just have a piece of my yummy cake already!"

Everyone burst out laughing.

"OK," said Jerry, pointing to the cake, "Let's all dig in now and satisfy our hungry souls." The crowd headed straight for the cake.

"Hey, Rabbi!" Jerry winked to me, "I even used the word soul! You must be rubbing off on me!"

Identification and Relation:
Does The Soul Keep Its Personality in the Afterlife?

A few months went by without much contact with Jerry. I was busy trying to review some new revised plans for the shul building and my fundraising tactics, when I received exciting news: Jerry had another grandchild. Actually, to be more accurate, Jerry now had additional new grand*children*—twins! Jerry was ecstatic, of course, that his extended family was growing. I imagined it was especially significant to him, since he had grown up as an only child, without siblings or even cousins.

Yet, I was wary. I felt that tug of my promise to Morris. Jerry had said Kaddish several times since the *shivah* period. The birth of these grandchildren provided yet another challenge. I wondered if Jerry's daughter was willing or interested in naming one of the twins after Morris. While Jerry and his father obviously had their differences, I was pretty confident that Jerry would want to honor his father by suggesting that his daughter name one of her twins after Morris.

Jerry called me at my home to come over and speak to him about this matter. I was there in a flash.

This time, when I arrived at Jerry's house, I was struck by how Jerry had aged since his father's passing. He was beginning to look just like his father. The wise eyes and the silver hair. Here was a new senior-looking Jerry, sitting in his recliner, smoking a pipe just like his father had before him.

Jerry was deep in thought and concerned. He began speaking to me slowly, as he playfully released the smoke through his nose.

"Rabbi, before our beautiful new children are named tomorrow," he said, "I need to ask you a few more questions about our soul conversation."

"Sure, Jerry: shoot!" I was thrilled. This was a good sign for me that Jerry was getting engaged in our discussion.

"Rabbi, remember what you said to me about my father's soul being an indestructible part of the Divine, and how after death his soul returned to its source? That really struck a chord with me. I have given it lots of thought and you know what? It generally makes good sense."

I nodded, wondering where the conversation would go.

"But Rabbi, there's something troubling about it. Assuming the soul *does* return to its origins, does that mean that my father is swallowed up into some greater entity, losing his individual identity forever? I just can't bear the thought of that. I've been tossing and turning for many nights thinking about the dreadful conclusion to your otherwise reasonable logic, Rabbi. While it's very comforting to know that my father exists as a spirit somewhere out in the cosmos, I'm fearful that I may have lost my chances to reconnect with him."

It seemed, as I listened, that Jerry was worried that even if his father Morris's spirit lived on, he was questioning whether Morris would keep his unique personality, and whether Jerry would ever have the chance to enjoy again the outstanding, intimate, and personal relationship he had shared with his father for a good part of his lifetime. Jerry was asking a profound philosophical question: Do souls maintain their personality and relationships with their family even after death?

Knowing Jerry, especially in light of all the unfinished business he had with his father, I could appreciate why this would worry him.

This whole issue reminded me of the pop song written by the iconic American singer, Eric Clapton. When Clapton's own son tragically fell out of the window of his fifty-third-story Manhattan apartment, he composed a song, *Tears in Heaven*, in his son's memory. The first line of the song is "Would you know my name if I saw you in Heaven?" It seems that Clapton, too, wondered if his son would still recognize him in the afterlife, and remember and appreciate their unique father-son relationship.

"Want to see the twins, Rabbi?" Jerry fumbled with his phone to bring up a picture of the adorable newborn twins.

"What do you say, Rabbi: Cute, eh?" Jerry was all smiles. "One of them even reminds me of my father, with that mischievous look."

I looked at the picture of these twins and couldn't help but get a bit *verklempt*. Here were the descendants of my Holocaust survivor friend Morris, who was almost written off from the human race by the Nazis, and here I am honored to witness the continuity of his family tree, against all odds!

I took the phone in my hands to see several more pictures of the babies. "These children are truly a miracle, Jerry. An absolute wonder!"

"Yes, Rabbi!" said Jerry, teary-eyed. "I just can't believe it! My family, as you know, was earmarked for the crematorium, and here we have in front of our eyes not just one, but two breathtaking miracles!" Jerry echoed my thoughts.

"Rabbi, I recall distinctly a similar sentiment that my mother, may she be well, shared with me on my wedding day."

"My son," she confided in me just before I walked down the aisle to my wedding canopy, "were it not for you, I would have given up hope a long time ago. It was you, my little Jerry, who brought a ray of light into our very dark lives.

"After the war, your father and I were totally broken, as can be expected. Even our marriage to each other, which was meant to be a happy occasion, was a story of two lonely, forlorn people offering company to each other in their misery. Our marriage had nothing to do with love or intimacy. It was basically two very sad people coming together to comfort each other.

"I remember how your father and I were crying all night long on our wedding night, thinking about how lucky we were to survive and about the tragic destiny of our poor families who perished in the Holocaust, and whose presence was palpably missing.

"One day, a few months later, looking at myself in the mirror in the privacy of my bedroom, I noticed my tattooed number from Auschwitz seared into the arm of my poor mutilated body. I recalled how the cursed concentration camp had turned a dazzling beauty into a skeleton: when we were liberated, I had lost so much of my hair, my face was scarred, several teeth had been knocked out, and I was thin as a rail. I now recalled the first time I saw myself in the mirror then, when I had cried, 'Oh G–d, *why*? *Why* did I deserve this? How had such a beautiful girl, who once had the most striking blonde hair and blue eyes, turned into this?'

"But now, a miracle had happened. I looked at myself again and gasped! Could it be true? I was lactating. Incredible! I had received my answer from G–d! I said to myself, 'From which unknown place in my dried out being is this new luscious life flowing from? Is it possible that such a worn out, broken, and abused body could possibly have rejuvenated? This is nothing less than a modern-day miracle: the revival of the dead!

"Then and there, it dawned on me that there was hope, just when I'd thought that all hope was gone. Indeed, life and happiness can return to the very same place that, not so many days ago, had been a receptacle of death and sadness. I now saw that it was time for me, Anna Goldstein, to get out of my depression and embrace the new life growing within me....

"It was only when I fell pregnant with you, Jerry, our '*Kaddishel*,' that things changed."

"Rabbi, those were my mother's emotional words to me, describing her pregnancy with me many years ago. And now, so many years later, I too, am experiencing the same thing with my children and even grandchildren. When I look into the eyes of these little newborn twins, they revive me. They bring me hope for the future. I find looking at them highly therapeutic. These little children, they release me from the clutches of sadness and despair, and they help me get over the loss of my father."

Both Jerry and I went off into this meditative trance, deeply moved by the power of destiny unfolding before our very own eyes. We felt overwhelmed by it. It was silent in the room for quite a long time.

Finally, Jerry broke the silence with a long sigh, and I gathered my thoughts to speak.

"You need to understand," I explained to Jerry, "that the human soul is not merely some nebulous energy without personality, animating the body. The soul always possessed, even prior to its birth, a distinct personality that defined it. And just like the soul itself is indestructible, its personality, too, is indestructible and forever," I assured him.

"Personality? A soul has personality?" asked Jerry. "I thought that our personality stems from the physical brain, our DNA and colorful life experiences!"

"The soul, too, contributes significantly to our personality as we know it. I mean, look at your grandchildren who are barely seven days old with hardly any physical development. Yet I can already see personality in the photos."

I recalled and shared a classic joke about Jewish parenting:

A Jewish mother is pushing her two baby boys in the double stroller when she runs into a friend of hers.

"They're so cute," coos the friend.

"How old are they?"

The mother beams. "The doctor is two," she replies promptly, "and the lawyer is one."

"Yes," I continued, "the physical DNA, hormones, and chemistry contribute, to a large degree, to the development of our personality, but even before the physical body kicks in, the soul arrives at birth with its own developed, distinct personality that is very much responsible for who we are. Before we were born there was already a conscious soul with a unique individual personality waiting to be dispatched to its assigned body."

"But Rabbi" insisted Jerry, "How can you be so convinced that the soul has a predetermined personality? Don't you think it makes more sense to say the soul merely animates the body with some generic life force or electricity, but the individual personality actually comes from our interaction with the world around us?"

"I hear you, Jerry, but just speak to any parent of a newborn and they will gladly offer to tell you all about their clever children and how they are convinced beyond the shadow of a doubt that their children exhibited a discernible personality and even a touch of " attitude" from the moment they were born! And Jerry, I am not speaking here about the aspirations and dreams that parents tend to hallucinate about their children prematurely, imagining their children possessing this perfect personality in their dream world. I am speaking about objective personality traits that parents claim to identify in their children from the moment they are born!"

"Again Rabbi, I don't mean to be disrespectful. But still, maybe it's the DNA that is present in every cell of the child from just after conception that accounts for the individual personality?" Jerry prodded.

I then looked at the photos of the identical twins, and said to Jerry:

"And how do you explain the very different personalities of your own daughter's twins, who share an identical DNA genome? How do you account for that? I am sure that you have already noticed some subtle personality differences between them?

"Let me tell you, Jerry, that over the course of many years as a rabbi, I have had the opportunity of speaking to many other parents of identical twins like these, who claim that—without any shadow of a doubt—their children have shown unique personalities and individual attitude from the day they were born. We are talking here about twins with identical DNA, Jerry. There are no physical differences in these children to account for their diverse personalities. How can we explain these differences? If these twins are truly identical, where do their personality differences come from?"

"Well, I can think of a number of things, Rabbi," said Jerry, who seemed to be taken aback by my practical arguments. "I recently read, Rabbi, in some reputable scientific journals, that the differences in identical twins can be attributed to the different experiences the twins may have experienced in the womb and at childbirth."

"Yes, I know, Jerry, about those outlandish theories," I replied. "But come on: You are a shrewd businessman. How can you buy into that nonsense? I can even hear in your own voice that you are not really convinced at all. And for a good reason. Scientists themselves have been baffled by this unusual phenomenon for years and have given all kinds of unusual desperate explanations. But it just doesn't add up. The simplest explanation that is straightforward and plausible—and, most importantly, it resonates with the parents that I have interviewed—is that the twins have different souls and their diverse dispositions and differences flow from their unique soul personalities that predated any interaction with their bodies!"

"Come to think of it, Rabbi," said Jerry, looking at the picture of his angelic little grand-twins, "you are definitely onto something! These kids were born with such personality!"

Jerry continued looking at the pictures of the twins. "OK, Rabbi, so let me ask you a general question about this soul-personality you talk about. If all souls ultimately come from the same source, the simple breath of G–d, how is it possible then to morph into such complex diverse personalities before ever meeting up with their physical body?"

"Good question, Jerry. The masters of the Kabbalah teach us that not only the soul but, in fact, every speck or particle emanating from the Divine has character and personality. In fact, the entire spiritual cosmos is made up of ten basic building blocks, known as the 'ten *sefirot*'—the spiritual DNA, so to speak—the ten attributes of G–d. How these attributes inter-play and interact with each other determines the individual personality of any given spiritual entity, and especially the human soul."

"Ten attributes, Rabbi? Only ten? *That* is what make people so diverse? I don't see how merely ten attributes can explain the complex people I have encountered over the years. And Rabbi," Jerry smiled, "I have met some really complicated creatures!"

"Take another good look at the faces of your gorgeous children." They really were such adorable kids that I just couldn't take my eyes off their perfect angelic faces! "Isn't it just amazing, Jerry, how only a few simple facial features like the eyes, nose, and mouth, can produce an infinite amount of distinctly differ-ent faces amongst the millions of people in the world?

"The same is true with the soul. Only ten simple attributes have infinite possibilities, and together they can morph into myriads of distinct soul personalities!

"And just like the divine soul itself, its personality, too, predates the soul's descent and fateful rendezvous with the body and all the earthly experiences that follow. This is the personality that parents can readily identify in their newborn babies, and it is this personality that distinguishes your one son from his identical sibling from the moment they were born!

In fact, the names that your children will give the twins at the baby naming ceremony during the circumcision is, according to the Kabbalah, a reflection of this predated soul personality that arrives at childbirth."

"Yes, Rabbi? Is that so?" Jerry perked up and straightened himself out on his chair. I could see that I had just said something that really sparked his interest.

"But how can it be, Rabbi, that a name given arbitrarily by the parents can reflect the predated individual personality belonging to that soul when the parents are choosing it with their limited human intelligence, in the best case, or more than likely simply out of a hat?" Jerry asked.

"The name that is given by the parents to a child after its birth belonged to that child's soul before the child was born, and it is not some random selection made by the parents. It is a true reflection of the personality of the soul." I explained.

"But how is that possible?" countered Jerry. "If the child is only given the name by parents who were never taught the pre-elected name or given any prior information on the origins of this soul?"

"The masters of the Kabbalah explain that baby naming is nothing less than a form of modern-day prophecy. When parents look into their baby's eyes, they can perceive their baby's soul and accurately uncover the preexisting name and soul-personality that belong to their newborn child from the beginning of time," I shared.

"Well, Rabbi, to be honest with you," said Jerry, "that's really why I called you to come meet me in the first place. I hope my daughter will name one of the twins after my father."

I nodded, leaning in closer to Jerry.

"Please be honest with me, Rabbi. Does a naming after a deceased person link the soul of the child to the deceased person they are named after and does the deceased know about the naming and still care?" Jerry asked.

"The Kabbalah writes that when naming a child after a loved one, the soul of the deceased is honored and elevated by that tribute, and an inseparable bond is then formed between the two souls," I answered. "Yes, the soul cares."

"Does that mean that my father will feel a sense of affinity to this child?" Jerry pressed.

"Yes, the shared name creates an intimate bond on the deepest levels of the soul," I assured him.

"Does that also mean that Dad will then watch over my little grandson and become his guardian angel?"

"Certainly, Jerry!"

"But do you really believe, Rabbi, that it is even remotely possible for my father's soul, after a traumatic death experience, to remember and relate to his old personality, and to his old earthly relationships?" Jerry asked. "And even if the soul does remember, don't you think that there is a reasonable possibility that the soul may voluntarily choose to forget its turbulent life on earth, so that it can move on to its new tranquil existence without the negative memories of the past?"

"I hear your point, Jerry, but the soul can never forget its individuality because this soul's personality that we are born with is an essential part of the soul. It will remain intact, even posthumously."

"The soul and its personality are not like two separate entities that can lose each other. The personality is not a garment that the soul dons and removes. The soul and the personality together constitute one and the same entity," I tried to clarify.

Jerry nodded. "Keep going, Rabbi. I really want to understand this."

"You have a valid concern. In fact, the idea of a soul desiring to escape its past is addressed by an ancient Jewish ritual performed by the burial society, the *Chevrah Kadisha*, just after death. As part of the extensive burial ritual and honors we give to the dead, a member of this secretive society says to the deceased, just before the casket is closed, "Don't forget that your Hebrew name is…""

"Yes, Rabbi," piped in Jerry. "I was there when they said that to Dad just before the funeral, and I was spooked out!"

"The reason, Jerry, for this spooky-sounding ritual is precisely to address your concern that after death, when the soul transitions into the next reality, it will be blown away by its new experiences and tempted to give up its past identity. Think of it like a powerful rock concert where one just wants to be lost in the crowd. The soul, too, instinctively wants to be absorbed in the Divine and lose its past identity and personality! It has many reasons to want to do so, but again, it just can't.

"Hence, the need to remind the soul of its unique name that symbolizes the soul's individual personality that it ultimately cannot escape from!"

"But Rabbi," Jerry then asked, "at the end of the day, even after this stern warning from the burial society, who says that in the scheme of things its personality is really so important? Why shouldn't the soul have the option, if it wants, to disengage itself from its personality and past?"

"The soul cannot divorce itself from its personality because the soul's individual personality is an indispensable part of the big picture. It ties into the cosmic plan for this specific soul — its unique mission that comes from up High. We are talking about its irreplaceable contribution to the ultimate plan." I hoped I was clarifying and not adding confusion.

Jerry motioned for me to continue speaking.

"You see, the Kabbalah teaches us that there are 600,000 general souls—all the souls of humanity—corresponding with the number of Jews that left Egypt. Each soul is endowed with a unique character, suited to help fulfill the collective human mission. Each individual soul plays a role in the universal overarching mission of fixing this world and turning it into a suitable home for the Divine. Each soul is endowed with unique talents and personality traits to help it successfully play its essential role in the collective mission. Without the participation of any one of the 600,000 individual souls and if there is a failure to engage any soul's unique talent and personality traits, the collective mission remains incomplete and the purpose of creation unfulfilled. This is why not just the soul, but its personality, too, is indestructible and lives on forever, just like the very soul itself, because of its crucial and irreplaceable individual role in completing the big picture."

"Wow, Rabbi, that's a really cool idea!" Jerry exclaimed.

I looked at my watch and realized I had to rush to an appointment with the president of my congregation. I wondered what news he had to share, what the destiny of our warm community would be. "What *is* the soul-mission of my little synagogue?" I wondered to myself, as I gripped Jerry in a bear hug and headed out the door.

The Circumcision Ceremony

A few days later, the big event took place. The greatly anticipated circumcision ceremonies of Jerry's boys was about to happen. Lisa, Jerry's wife, had insisted on hosting it at their home so their daughter could rest and get some help with the babies. Just like at the memorial breakfast for Morris, everyone who was a "somebody" made sure to be there. Jerry knew how to pull in the crowds. Some arrived because they wanted to impress the influential business tycoon, while others came without any agenda, to simply bring good wishes to their friend on his special day.

I watched Jerry as he remained immersed in the moment, completely focused on his grandchildren as the sacred circumcision ritual was performed on the twins. I was honored with the baby naming. As I read the prayers and, at the request of Jerry's son-in-law, officially named one of the boys after Jerry's father, announcing Jerry's father's Hebrew name, Moishe, Jerry completely lost it. The usually controlled and composed Jerry began sobbing uncontrollably. You could see that it touched him to his very core.

In general, there is no greater inner satisfaction than knowing that your father's name is being perpetuated in this world by your own kin. For Jerry, this was an opportunity to make amends with his estranged father. The prophetic nature of baby naming only added to the emotional volcano that we all witnessed erupting in his soul.

I approached Jerry to calm him down. I embraced him and patted him on his back until his crying subsided. Jerry's intense reaction ignited my own feelings toward Morris, my hero. I felt relieved that Jerry's family had memorialized him, eternalizing his name in this new being. I had kept part of my pact with Morris, at least. Then I felt my own tears rise to my eyelids, and I reached for a tissue as I tried to compose myself, too.

Later, during the cocktails, Jerry cornered me with a drink in his hand and asked, "Rabbi, do you think that one day when I meet up with my father he will thank my family for this?"

"What do you mean, Jerry?"

"For naming my grandson after him?"

"Sure, Jerry."

And then, after a long pause, Jerry opened his heart, asking me another question.

"And do you honestly think, Rabbi, that when I meet up with him on that important day, I will still recognize him? Even without his body?"

"Sure, Jerry! He may not have a body, but there is always his soul that you will surely know!"

"But Rabbi, how will I possibly recognize him as a soul if he has no body?"

"Jerry, in Heaven you will know your father not by his physical features, but by his soul personality that we spoke about before. His colorful personality that lives on as part of his soul; his character traits that you have familiarized yourself with over the years—they will guide you! Just like you knew your father's presence and personality down here on earth without physically touching or seeing him, you will know your father's soul personality in Heaven when you encounter him! It's like a blind person finding someone by using their sense of smell!"

"OK, Rabbi, but that still sounds a little obscure. Is there anything else that you can offer me to help me track down my father's soul?"

"Yes, there is more, Jerry."

"There's another important distinguishing factor to look out for in identifying the soul of a loved one. It is known as the soul's "garments.""

"Garments of the soul? What are those, Rabbi?"

"Our tradition teaches us that every good deed we do in this world unleashes a creative force—an angel of positive energy. Conversely, every sin we commit unleashes a destructive force—a negative angel. These angels are our true legacy. They belong to us. They have our name written all over them. We are their masters because we created them. When we die, these angels escort us and surround us. They even attend our funeral, to claim a stake in our spiritual legacy!"

"After we die and our soul arrives in Heaven, it is escorted by these angels—both the positive and negative ones. They herald us into Heaven and surround us. Then they continue to serve as the soul's respective advocates and prosecutors in the heavenly tribunal. Subsequently, after a period of judgment, the soul is purged of its negative angels, who are by nature transient, and the soul is then left exclusively with the positive angels, representing the acts of kindness and piety performed in the course of our lifetime. These angels remain with us eternally. They reflect our life's true achievements and collectively form a glowing aura around the soul. This is known in the mystical texts as the "garments" or the "crown" of the soul."

The aura and glow of these angels embellish the soul and serve as a further means to identify the soul by its lifetime crown of achievements and good deeds. All of a person's positive accomplishments achieved throughout their years on earth are reflected in the royal attire embellishing the soul.

So there you go, Jerry. Your dad's soul can be easily identified by his outstanding soul personality, and if that doesn't cut it, he can also be identified by the luminous aura surrounding his soul, representing the long list of his lifelong accomplishments in this world."

"Incredible, Rabbi. I have never heard this from anyone else and it really speaks to me!" Jerry exclaimed. He then spontaneously raised his glass to all the guests and proposed a toast:

"My friends, my truly good friends who have come from far and wide to celebrate in this very joyous occasion, let us now propose a toast to the newborn babies who have just entered into the covenant of Israel! To the twins—the new little souls. How honored we are today to have given one of the children a name in honor of my father! May this young precious boy and his brother both merit to live up to their namesakes! I am sure that my father, Morris, is very pleased with this honor bestowed upon him today. While Dad and I may have had our differences—as you all know, especially in the last few years—

I requested that one of the babies be given his name, and I am grateful to my daughter and son-in-law for honoring my request. It gives me great pleasure to offer Dad this gesture of reconciliation! I hope you appreciate this, Dad, wherever you are! *L'chaim*—to life!"

Everyone clapped and toasted Jerry, the babies, and his entire clan. Jerry's mother and wife beamed. I whispered a thank you to G–d, hoping that Morris's soul could hear.

Picking Up the Pieces

Jerry kept in touch for a few weeks after his grandsons' circumcision. I felt that we were developing an almost brotherly bond, checking in daily about the joys of being a grandfather of these latest additions to the family. I thought Morris would be proud of me. I hoped I had helped mend the rift between father and son.

The person I worried about more and more was Morris's wife, Anna. She was frail, and she had been very quiet lately. Anna seemed sad behind her elegant clothing and perfectly coiffed hair. My wife, Chana, had tried reaching out a few times, but the conversation had stayed at the surface level. Finally, I decided to bring up this topic to Jerry. Maybe there was a way to comfort her.

"I'm worried about my mother, too," Jerry said, wrinkling his brow. "It seems that my father was the glue that kept our family together. None of us are the same without him."

"It's a big, life-changing loss," I said, leaning closer to show support. Jerry had dropped by my office at the synagogue when he heard I was concerned about his mom. We sat in the cozy, familiar room surrounded by books and pictures. It was the first time since Morris passed away that Jerry had come to visit me here, at the building I'd poured my heart into for thirty years. If he was shocked at the leak-stained ceiling and other aspects of the aging building, Jerry didn't let on. Instead, surprisingly, he picked up our soul conversation.

"It must be so hard on my mom. I was thinking about what you said, that it is possible to reconnect after death, and even maintain a special kinship. I wonder if my mother has that longing and need as well. It makes me wonder if my father is still going to be my dad. Will we still be the Goldstein family? Will we ever connect again in the intimate way that parents relate to their children in this world?"

"Of course, Jerry," I answered. "Relatives are not just physically connected. Their souls are related, too."

"All family members?" Jerry asked.

"Souls of parents continue to connect with their children even after death. The children continue to help their parents in the afterlife by doing good deeds on their behalf, and the parents continue to watch over their children from up high," I told him. "Spouses are together forever, and siblings, too, remain intimately connected even after death."

"I don't get how we can remain related after our bodies are buried, Rabbi. We're related because of our DNA," Jerry questioned.

"We are related on a deeper soul level too," I said. "Regarding the souls of husbands and wives, the marriage connection, the Talmud says that forty days before a child is born a voice calls out from the heavens saying that the son of so and so shall marry the daughter of such and such. Implicit in this heavenly announcement is that the relationship between a husband and wife predates their birth. Even before they were born and introduced to their bodies and their DNA, these couples belonged to each other."

Jerry looked at me with skepticism, but he motioned for me to continue. I took my cue and kept speaking, hoping my words from the heart would support Jerry.

"The Kabbalah takes this idea a step further and says that a husband and wife were once actually two halves of the very same soul. Jerry, I am sure you are familiar with the term *soul mates*?" I said.

"Of course," he said.

"The belief in soul mates is that it is identical to the physical creation of the bodies of Adam and Eve, who were initially created as one being and only at a later time were cut at the rib to create two separate beings—male and female. Likewise, on the spiritual level, it is the belief that every husband and wife were once a part of a single soul that was split in half, and both halves were sent down on earth to find each other," I explained. "From this perspective, finding one's spouse and marrying them is not some new discovery. It is husband and wife reclaiming their original half-soul and reuniting."

Jerry wasn't satisfied with this answer. "But how do we know, Rabbi, that this soul connection to a spouse remains even after death?" he asked.

"If they were soul mates before birth don't you think it is logical that they should remain mates after death?" I challenged.

"I knew dad's passing would be hard on my mother," Jerry pondered. "But I didn't realize she was a part of him. How does it work for the relationship between a parent and child?"

"Jerry, we are taught that parents remain very much connected and involved with their children even after they die. For instance, we have a lesser-known tradition, recorded in the Talmud, that pious deceased parents may choose to visit their children on the weekends," I said, wondering if he would find this horrifying or hilarious.

The Talmud records that, after his death, Rabbi Yehudah the prince used to visit his home, wearing Sabbath clothes, every Friday evening at dusk. He would recite the Kiddush prayers. One Friday night there was a knock at the door. "Sorry," said the maid, "I can't let you in just now because Rabbi Yehudah is in the middle of Kiddush." From then on, he stopped coming, since he did not want his coming to become public knowledge.

"C'mon, Rabbi, that sounds a bit over the top," Jerry chuckled. "I don't know if I could handle that."

"This is mystical stuff, Jerry. Then there is the more common belief that the souls of loved ones return to earth to their living relatives on special holidays, too. As you surely know there is a famous memorial prayer, known as Yizkor, recited on the main Jewish holidays by those who have lost a loved one, remembering their souls," I shared.

"Yes, that's the time when all the children have to wait outside the sanctuary," Jerry added. "That was my favorite part of the holiday service, growing up."

I smiled, picturing young Jerry tugging on his father's prayer shawl. "Tradition has it that there is a great uproar in the heavens at that time because all these old souls are dressing up and going to visit their children down on earth for the special holiday prayer," I added.

Jerry smiled, staring off into nowhere.

"On a more positive note, there is also a tradition, Jerry, that the deceased parents, grandparents, and great-grandparents of a bride and groom come from their heavenly abode to join in at the wedding celebration of their progeny. I have spoken with many couples who claim that they were able to perceive the presence of their ancestors at their own wedding, and it was so palpable that it felt as if they were standing right beside them under the wedding canopy."

"I don't know if that's cool or creepy, Rabbi," said Jerry.

"My point is that all of these traditions add up to the overall belief that the family bond stays intact, and relatives remain very much related, even after death. The souls of parents continue to watch over the lives of their children and grandchildren; they continue to derive pride (or conversely, pain) from their children's deeds and accomplishments, and they intercede on their children's behalf before the heavenly throne. The same applies not only to children but also to all those with whom the soul was connected in its lifetime through bonds of love, friendship, and community," I said, hoping to pull all these lofty and mystical ideas together into something meaningful for Jerry.

"It's a lot to think about, Rabbi," Jerry said. "That's what I like about our conversations. It takes everything to a deeper level."

"After death, because the soul is no longer constricted by the limitations of the physical body, its relationships are in many ways, even closer, deeper, and more meaningful than ever before," I continued.

"I hear what you are saying" said Jerry, sounding comforted. "I am pleased to know that my father and I will remain family. But to me, family is not just about some merely DNA-based familial bond; it's also the shared memories. What do you think, Rabbi: Does the soul also remember the outlandish times it spent together with us here on earth—the good times and the bad? If and when I will meet up with my father once again, will we truly remember each other as we were in the good old days? Will there be the shared sense of nostalgia? Will we have the capacity to sit down once again and *shmooze* wherever our conversation left off on earth?

"I guess what I'm really asking, Rabbi, is: Does the soul of the deceased still keep its "memory card," even after it leaves behind its physical brain? And is it even possible at all for this lofty spirit, removed from the physical body, to still relate in the afterlife to its old, trivial memories of a world that it has graduated from a long time ago?" Jerry added.

"In the other world, there is no forgetting at all, Jerry," I replied. "Forgetfulness is an *earthly* condition. In the afterlife, everything is remembered. We learn this from a famous prayer that reads: "For there is no forgetfulness before You," I explained.

Jerry nodded, and motioned for me to continue.

"Did you ever wonder why there is a natural indentation on your face, on your upper lip?" I pointed to the lips on the picture of the cute newborns on Jerry's keychain and explained that I was using the kids for my demonstration and I couldn't really display my own, because of the thick mustache and beard covering my face.

"Not really, Rabbi. But now I'm curious. What *does* it mean?" he asked.

"There is a legend in the Talmud that, before a child is born, when it is still in utero, the child is taught the entire Bible by an angel. Then, just before the child is born, the angel taps the child on the lip—creating the indent—and all the knowledge is forgotten."

"Rabbi, that's wild," Jerry commented.

"Isn't it? The point is that forgetfulness is introduced to the soul for the very first time at *childbirth*. Because forgetfulness doesn't exist in Heaven. It is a human condition, not a heavenly one," I added.

"Well, it's a shame that our soul powers can't erase forgetfulness. It would be so useful," Jerry said, chuckling. "My wife would never hassle me when I forget to take the garbage out, or I forget to buy the right things from the grocery store."

"Actually, forgetfulness was given to us fragile humans as a gift, to help us deal with our seemingly endless problems and pain. It was given to us as a coping mechanism. Because honestly, if we were to remember at any given moment all our problems and issues, we would never cope. If we remembered all the intense pain we endured over the years, would we ever have a moment of peace in our lives?" I explained. "But you do have a point."

Jerry laughed.

"If we, or our wives, remembered all our grudges and held

on to them, we would literally explode. We need to forget them and let go, as the expression goes: 'forgive and forget'! Every night before we go to sleep, Jewish tradition tells us to recite a special prayer about releasing ourselves from all our grudges," I said.

I saw Jerry's eyes light up. I felt I had hit a nerve.

"Is that a fact that every night we need to off-load our grudges, Rabbi?" Jerry asked pensively. "Over the last few years I could have used that prayer many times."

This time I was the one nodding for Jerry to continue.

"You know" said Jerry, getting very serious, "I don't know what happened to completely destroy my relationship with my father. We tried many times to make up, but it never was quite the same. You know there was nothing my father wouldn't do for me, but we could never get it back on track. Boy, do I have loads of grudges sitting very heavily right on my heart."

"All of us do, Jerry," I said, thinking of the various people who had hurt me over the years. It was hard to be a rabbi, some-times, delivering uncomfortable news to people, trying to offer support and comfort, and fundraising for projects that were important to me, but not necessarily to the people I needed and hoped would support me. "I try and tell myself people are just doing the best they can, even if their words or actions are not kind to me, or helpful. Sometimes I run into people who were unkind, and they appear to have no idea that they have wronged me. Or sometimes people avoid me, and I may not realize what I have done to wrong them. Either way, time can help soften the grudges. And eventually, forgetfulness helps us let go of our grudges and move on."

"I don't know, Rabbi," Jerry interrupted. "I can forgive, but I was raised by Holocaust survivors who taught me to never forget."

"You're, right, Jerry. We sometimes misuse this gift of forgetfulness by forgetting that which is important as well. Like conveniently forgetting those who generously helped us, like our parents, or callously forgetting to study our family or community history, and as a result, repeating the same mistakes of history over and over again. Or how about forgetting the very G–d that gave us the gift of forgetfulness in the first place?" I explained. Jerry's point was important, and I wanted to explore it.

"It is hard for me to imagine that any good can result from forgetfulness," Jerry interjected.

"That is why great books like the Bible speak about the importance of remembering, and not forgetting, over and over again, addressing this unfortunate human ungratefulness and mega-abuse of the gift of forgetfulness," I conceded. "But there is also a positive side to forgetfulness, which gives us the ability to let go of our past grievance. This type of forgetfulness might just soften your last few years of acrimony and noncommunication with your father.

"But what will I accomplish?" asked Jerry. "Even if I go ahead like you are advising me — to be proactive and to let go of my grievances, my father himself, who you said never forgets in the afterlife, will continue holding on to his grievances against me forever. What's the benefit of me forgiving and forgetting, if he will continue being angry at me? How do I know that he won't punish me? And Rabbi, when I meet up with him in the afterlife, who is to say that he will not still be aggrieved and irreconcilable?" Jerry was speaking loudly now. I was afraid for a moment he would erupt in anger, but his movements remained smooth and calm.

"Jerry," I responded, gazing at his silhouette against the blue sky, "We believe the afterlife to be a world of truth, a place where the soul is enlightened, and it regrets its former pettiness and closedmindedness. It would be safe to assume that the souls would drop their grievances as well."

"But what if my father may have had a valid reason to disown me?" Jerry burst out. This was the first time I'd heard him accept any responsibility for the painful rift. "Can he still drop his grievances and embrace me from Heaven? After all, I did show him disrespect," Jerry said with pain.

"Listen, Jerry, no reason is good enough to hold on to our grievances indefinitely," I said calmly, "especially if you are remorseful. I am sure that your merciful father will consider pardoning you, his one and only son."

"That's a relief," Jerry said, speaking quietly now. "I had not realized until now how much I want peace with my father, how much I want him to forgive. I even miss the old guy."

I wanted to lean over and give Jerry a hug. He seemed to be introspective and vulnerable now. He had accepted some measure of responsibility for the fight with his father and wanted closure. I wished I could provide some kind of tangible resolution. I missed Morris more than I had in a long time, and I felt his presence in the space between Jerry and me. Was his soul watching us right now? That much, I didn't know.

Destination:
Where Does the Soul Go?

What Is Heaven?
And Do We Believe In Hell?

I was sitting down to prepare a lecture for my weekly Torah class when Jerry called. A week had passed since our last conversation, and I wondered how Jerry and his mother were doing. While I had a lot to do, I welcomed the interruption.

"Are you afraid of flying a plane, Rabbi?" he asked. "Um," I hesitated, "Possibly. Why?"

"You know that, for me, flying a plane is not just a hobby; it's a passion."

"Yes, Jerry," I said. "You've mentioned how much you enjoy flying. It must be an amazing feeling to guide an aircraft into the sky. How can I help? I certainly can't help with the flying," I laughed. I heard Jerry chuckle over the phone.

"Rabbi, if you would only agree, I would love to take you out for a spin over downtown Ottawa, to show you how beautiful the world looks from up in the air. It would be a great honor for me to share with you, my rabbi, one of my life's greatest pleasures. I feel like up high, in the sky, I'll be closer to my father," he said, offering me a unique invitation. I was intrigued, and a little stressed, wondering whether or not to abandon my sermon-writing for some fun. Flying with Jerry was a once-in-a-lifetime adventure.

"Of course, Jerry, I would love to join you," I replied instantly. Even though, truth be told, I am dead scared of flying a small, one-engine plane—no matter how luxurious—I would never miss the opportunity to support Jerry in his healing process.

I made my way over to the small, wind-blown airport to meet up with Jerry.

"Rabbi, am I glad to see you," Jerry said, as I walked with him onto the tarmac toward his luxurious small plane. "I miss my father so much. There is such a void in my heart."

I saw tears forming in his eyes as he continued speaking, more openly and emotionally than usual. "In the good old days, when my father and I were getting along, we would go out flying together regularly, just me and him every Sunday. This was another one of our special father-son private bonding times. Back then, I didn't know those times wouldn't last forever."

We boarded the plane together. Jerry sat in the captain's seat and invited me to sit next to him as co-captain. It was overwhelming to view the world from that powerful vantage point. The instruments looked complicated and made nervous beeping noises.

"Rabbi, I need to be near where my father is now. In my dreams, when I'm restless from grief all night, I believe his soul is up there, in the sky."

I listened to Jerry and watched his hands maneuver the many instruments. I tried to still my heart, which was racing faster and faster as we pulled onto the runway.

Jerry continued speaking, as if he wasn't about to launch us into the sky. "Rabbi, I understand what you taught me over the last few months, about the soul being an indestructible part of the Divine, and having an immortal personality and all of that. Those thoughts are all very comforting. But I still wonder: Where, exactly, did my father's soul go?"

I closed my eyes, as we lifted off the runway. "He's in Heaven, Jerry," I blurted.

Jerry was silent for a moment. "Heaven? You have got to be kidding," he said cynically. "Rabbi, you know me. I am a realist." He pointed up to the sky. "I know that the physical sky up there is real because I have been there and back many times, but a *spiritual* Heaven? Have you ever thought that, perhaps, you religious people have this all wrong and when you get up there, there's just nothing to be found—absolutely nothing? Or better yet, maybe when you come up there, a fancy black limo pulls up, and a guy in a three-piece suit gets out of the car and with great drama flashes you a sign that says, 'Sucker'?"

"That's creative," I said, "I never heard of a black limo version before."

The old Jerry was back—the practical business executive who rejected any vestige of a spiritual world. I wondered what had triggered Jerry's sudden strong reaction.

Then Jerry added, "Do you know of anyone who has gone there and come back to tell the story?"

Well, to be honest, this was not the first time I'd heard this question, but frankly, I hated it. True, I haven't been to Heaven recently, or at least I can't remember being there. But that doesn't mean Heaven doesn't exist. Last I heard, Honolulu still exists even though I have never been there, either. But I chose not to make that point. Instead I just addressed Jerry's challenge head-on:

"Jerry, think this through for a moment. If the soul is, as we discussed, an indestructible part of G–d with a unique personality replete with intelligence, emotions, and even memory, where do you think all of that disappears to in the afterlife? Obviously, at the moment of death—after the soul is dislodged from its physical body—it continues to move on to a higher sphere, closer to its origin, to a place we happen to call 'Heaven.' Where else, Jerry?"

"That's what I'm asking you, Rabbi," Jerry said. "What are the other options? Please keep going, but I'm not promising I'll ever buy into it."

"OK, I hear you. I have no expectations. Basically, without Heaven, this whole world is pointless and unjust. Without a Heaven, there is no reward for the good guys, and no punishment for the wicked. You see, life as we know it is an unfinished story. Paul Harvey, the famous radio announcer, coined the phrase, 'the rest of the story.' Jerry, *Heaven* is 'the rest of the story' of our lives."

"There must be other options, Rabbi," Jerry said skeptically. "It would be easier to settle scores in *this* world."

"If there was only this world, Jerry, without an afterlife, then all the rotten people like Hitler would just walk free, unpunished, and their tragic victims would remain unrewarded and never avenged. That would be a real shame."

"That is the first thing you've said about Heaven that I can possibly relate to," Jerry said. He glanced at me across the cockpit. While religion and G-d still spooked Jerry, avenging Hitler's victims was an idea he could relate to. The sky was blue and clear. I wondered if Morris's soul was witnessing Jerry and me soaring high above Ottawa.

"Without Heaven, we are left with no reasonable explanation as to why the good people in this world are constantly suffering, and why the wicked continue to prosper," I added. "The only plausible explanation is that there is more to this story in another life, where everything is evened out and all scores are settled. There needs to be a 'story after the story,' Jerry."

"It's a nice thought, Rabbi," said Jerry, fiddling with the instruments of the plane. "If all the scores could be settled, I'd feel more at peace."

"What you said reminds me of a story I heard in my rabbinic academy days," I told Jerry.

"Let's hear," he said, as he flicked the plane's machinery in preparation for our trip.

In the Russia of the 1920s, when the iron talons of the Soviet regime were determined to tear apart the remaining vestiges of Soviet Judaism, Rabbi Yosef Yitzchak Schneersohn (1880–1950) was mercilessly brutalized and tortured for his "counterrevolutionary" activities — the creation of an underground network of yeshivahs, mikvahs and other banned Jewish institutions.

Time and again, the Rebbe was dragged into the interrogation room. In the dank darkness, where brutes and cutthroats were regularly brought to their knees, the Rebbe openly defied these savages. It was on one such occasion that one of the Rebbe's interrogators pointed a revolver at the Rebbe and smirked: "This toy has a way of making people cooperate."

Calmly, the Rebbe replied: "That toy is persuasive to one who has many gods and only one world; I have One G–d and two worlds."

Our wise teachers of yore understood that, for justice to exist, there must be a continuation to the story on earth in a future place they called Heaven," I added, my voice tired after talking over the noisy plane engines.

I was enjoying the conversation with Jerry so much that I almost forgot that I was sitting in the copilot seat in a single-engine plane 10,000 feet in the air. Now that we were at a comfortable altitude, overlooking the city from a very clear perspective, Jerry pointed out various historical landmarks. It was just like Jerry promised me: absolutely breathtaking to be looking down at the Canadian capital city on this beautiful, clear day.

The view distracted me from our conversation, yet Jerry didn't forget where we had left off.

"Rabbi, I also need you to explain something else that has always bothered me about Heaven. If I understand correctly, Heaven is supposed to be a place of great reward and pleasure. But how can that be if we believe that the afterlife is exclusively for souls without physical bodies? Aren't all pleasures connected in some way to the physical body? If we leave behind our primary enjoyer of pleasure—the body—what is left for the soul to enjoy? How can the soul alone possibly enjoy all the heavenly pleasures without a body?"

"Great question, Jerry." I said, pausing to formulate an answer.

Jerry kept talking. "Imagine if we had traveled up here in this plane to enjoy the amazing celestial scenery, and then you remembered that you left your glasses behind. It would be almost a total waste of your time, as you would be missing the necessary tool to appreciate and enjoy the beauty of the scenery."

"It would be an absolute shame!" I agreed.

"Rabbi, I know that in other religions they believe in a Heaven filled with sensual pleasures. They look forward to a great feast or even carnal gratification. Even though I strongly disagree with this notion of a 'juicy steak in Heaven,' at least that is something I can wrap my head around." Jerry added, adjusting the instruments of the plane.

"Jerry, do you know what I think Heaven really is? Obviously, it's not a place of *physical* pleasures, as it is impossible to have physical pleasure without a body. But it's also not necessarily a place of stereotypical spiritual pleasures either. To me, Heaven is something much deeper and practical," I explained.

"Practical?" Jerry asked. "How is Heaven practical?"

"In my mind, Heaven is a place where we are given a brand new, higher perspective on the life we just lived. It is like being given a pair of 3-D glasses. This new full-view perspective on life is the reward we have in store for us in the World to Come," I continued, watching Jerry manage the plane.

"What if I don't want the glasses?" Jerry asked. "What if I don't want to see what I have done: especially the things I have done wrong?"

"It's all about perspective, Jerry. I would describe Heaven as the marvelous view of the city from way up here in the plane. Look at our city. It is breathtaking! I can see the skyscrapers and the architecture of royal Ottawa like I have never seen them before," I answered. It was a good reminder to myself to look for the bigger picture of my own circumstances with my dwindling community and funds.

"This new perspective answers all our questions and gives us peace of mind," I added. "Let me explain this with a story."

> A young boy was watching his mother weaving a tapestry. It took her forever. One day, shortly before she finished, the boy picked it up and said to himself: "Mommy, forgive me— you may be the best mother in the world, but when it comes to needlework, well, this is a mess! There's a piece of red sticking out here. Over here, there's a turquoise thread that seems to go nowhere."
>
> The whole thing looked like chaos.
>
> Suddenly, his fingertips detected smooth regular stitching on the other side of the tapestry. He turned the tapestry over and saw the most beautiful sight: An exquisite and precise copy of Gainsborough's *Boy in Blue*. The stitches were so regular and well formed. The colors all blended so beautifully. A Divine tapestry! All the disjointed threads that he'd seen on the other side of the tapestry harmonized into a complete and beautiful whole.

"Nice, story, Rabbi," Jerry told me, patting my arm, as he continued steering the plane. "But it's difficult for me to imagine that everything really is positive."

"You see, while we live in the physical world, we were exposed to only a very limited one-dimensional perspective on life. All we see is the unfinished back of the tapestry. Handicapped by this limited view, we are confounded by life's mysteries and plagued by the many unanswered questions life presents us," I continued. "We are naturally distracted by the many seemingly disjointed threads that make up the fabric of life. All of the suffering and imbalances that we encounter, like the disjointed threads in the back of the tapestry, make life on earth seem like a very unfair and senseless experience," I explained.

Jerry nodded, zooming through a gentle cloud. I wondered how long we would stay up here, how long Jerry wanted this moment to last. We were both silent for a moment, enjoying the view of the city below us.

"Life does seem quite unfair, Rabbi," Jerry said after our pause. "There are so many issues that divide families, communities, and the world. It is difficult to understand why G–d would create a world with so much inequality and strife."

"In Heaven, we are granted a glimpse of the front side of the tapestry. We are given the missing logic behind all the disjointed threads. Seeing the tapestry of life gives us an appreciation for how each thread is essential, and how each one contributes to the overall beauty of the tapestry. In Heaven, we have an understanding of all the unsolved mysteries of this world. Up there, we can finally say, perhaps for the very first time: yes, there is a bigger picture, and yes, there truly is justice to this world," I continued. I leaned back in my copilot's bucket seat. I was starting to get hungry and began thinking about all my responsibilities back on the ground.

"Still, Rabbi," Jerry wondered aloud, "even if Heaven is enlightening, where is the pleasure in this?"

"Do you want to know how they experience pleasure in Heaven?" I asked. I felt like all my explaining was making the whole concept of Heaven even more confusing.

"Yeah, I do," Jerry said.

"OK, Jerry, just look down at the highway below us. It's rush hour now and, while it may be smooth sailing up here in the empty lanes of the celestial kingdom, down there below they are all sitting in frantic traffic and tension."

"Where are you going with this, Rabbi?" Jerry asked.

"Jerry, I am sure you must have, on many occasions, found yourself sitting in a traffic jam, frustrated and angry about your predicament. Then, out of sheer desperation, you turn on your radio and you hear your favorite traffic reporter in the helicopter reporting about the cause of the distressing delay you are experiencing."

"OK," Jerry said, "I've definitely been stuck in traffic before."

"Because the news reporter is positioned in his cushy helicopter above, he can comfortably tell you from his coveted vantage point that there is really no need to hyperventilate, and that your traffic jam is about to end. You can now take a sigh of relief, and thank the man in the sky for the good news."

"But why do we need to know after we've died?" Jerry questioned. "By then, it's too late to help down here in the present reality."

"What I mean is, panicking in this physical world is the result of being exposed to a limited perspective. When you are reintroduced to the very same set of circumstances, but this time from a higher perspective, suddenly everything changes and you can calm down and feel at peace," I tried, hoping I was making sense.

"It's hard to imagine feeling at peace about how I ended the relationship with my father," Jerry said quietly. "I have a lot of regrets lately. It keeps me up at night."

"I hear you, Jerry. I can only imagine your pain," I said sadly. Was all this explaining and philosophizing what Jerry needed? He was in pain, and grief could be a long process. What comforting words might possibly help?

"Rabbi, you have no idea," Jerry said, shaking his head back and forth.

"I guess even if you were to hear that the traffic up ahead is worse than you thought, you are still better off than before," I began, "because by simply knowing this information, you at least have a clear vision of what to expect, which empowers you, calms you down, and helps you take control of the situation. There's hope: that's what I'm trying to say."

"Thanks, Rabbi," Jerry said. "All that truth doesn't sound pleasurable, exactly."

"And yet, when we become privy to the heavenly perspective which gives us the total picture, we experience immense pleasure and joy from this newfound peace of mind, and we feel unbelievable serenity...." I told him.

"Have you ever heard the phrase, 'Let sleeping dogs lie'?" Jerry interrupted.

"Our sages teach us that there is no greater joy than the clarity achieved by the dispelling of doubts, Jerry," I shared. "When we finally get to Heaven and receive answers to all the questions that have plagued us for an entire lifetime, we are overtaken by a wave of inner contentment. This is the peace of mind and great pleasure in store for us in the World to Come."

"The sages wrote that when they were still alive," Jerry argued. "It still sounds so theoretical. I want to hear about real pleasure."

"To me, the most painful thing about this world is not so much the pain per se, but the nagging doubts and uncertainty that come with it," I said.

"Hold on, Rabbi," interrupted Jerry. "Pain hurts with or without the doubts that accompany it! Losing my father and watching him suffer so badly...Wasn't the pain awful enough, with or without the doubts that accompanied it?"

"Let me answer your question in the classical Jewish fashion—with another question to you: What would you say, Jerry, is the difference between the excruciating pain associated with the delivery of a baby and that of passing a kidney stone? Why is it that childbearing is considered a relatively tolerable pain, while passing stones is considered unbearable?"

"I don't know, Rabbi," Jerry said. "Did you speak to your wife about this example? She may not agree." He chuckled as he soared the plane higher.

"Very funny. In other words, Jerry, when we experience pain in the context of an overarching greater purpose, the pain is then greatly diminished. On the other hand, when we experience random pain with no apparent purpose, the pain is then unbearable."

"In Heaven there is no pain at all because the purpose of everything is so crystal clear. There is only pleasure and celebration of that clarity."

"I don't know," Jerry said. "I don't think I can handle all that clarity. It brings up too much pain."

"When you experienced your father's suffering, Jerry, from your perspective there was no apparent purpose or logic to it, and that's why it hurt so much," I explained.

Jerry looked pensive. "So do you think that when I get to Heaven and see things from the new perspective, I will be able to make some sense out of his suffering and his painful death?"

"Yes, Jerry, I believe you will. According to the sages, Heaven gives us logic to understand our suffering, and it even clarifies the dark mysteries of death. It is where all the pieces of the puzzle come together. If only we could train ourselves to see life from that heavenly perspective while living on earth! Then, wow, nothing would faze us, and we could have a piece of Heaven on earth," I answered, imagining what the purpose for my own struggles might be.

"Enough talking about this spiritual stuff, Rabbi." Jerry's voice sounded lighter, happier. "Let me show you what true Heaven on earth can be. Rabbi, you take the plane controls," Jerry said, examining the copilot controls near my seat.

"Are you serious? You really want me to fly this plane?" My hands were shaking at the thought.

"Of course, Rabbi, it's simple. You see that highway just below?" Jerry said confidently.

"Sure, Jerry." I looked below at the tiny cars and people. "I'm worried I won't know where to go, or which direction."

"Rabbi, what you do is follow the direction of the road as if you would be driving a car. It's as simple as that," he said with encouragement.

I took the steering wheel and followed the highway below, just like Jerry had suggested. My stomach dropped for a second, as I felt the plane yield to my control. I felt both vulnerable and powerful as I glided Jerry's beautiful plane. I thought about how Jerry's life was different from mine. He had every material advantage, which, it seemed to me, allowed him to let go and enjoy a moment like this: to see the beauty and splendor of the earth we were looking down upon. I could learn from his confidence, his ability to be present, to have fun. The stress of renovating my little congregation was crushing. I hadn't felt this light and free in months. Enjoying the moment had felt frivolous as the community I'd built for decades seemed to dwindle in size and enthusiasm. It was great fun gliding the plane in the clear blue skies while watching the people below snake through the afternoon traffic.

"Okay, Rabbi," Jerry said to me, getting back to our subject. "I understand on a general level what you have been saying about Heaven. But something still doesn't sit right with me."

"What do you mean, Jerry?" I asked. "What bothers you?"

"For example, do you really believe that there is a grand tribunal in Heaven, with a supreme judge sitting there who will judge us?"

I nodded, as Jerry continued.

"And is there an accounting made of our entire life in front of this tribunal with a balance sheet of our good deeds and sins presented? It seems like a childish notion," he added.

"Considering your difficult legal battle with your father, I can totally appreciate why you may be uncomfortable with the thought of yet another day in court," I said, turning the plane controls back to Jerry. "Thanks for letting me fly this beautiful plane," I added, grateful for that once-in-a-lifetime experience. The thrill of being up high, guiding such an elegant machine, was unforgettable.

"I'm glad you came, Rabbi," Jerry said, smiling. "And you were brave enough to give it a try."

I chuckled. "Yeah, that was the experience of a lifetime!" I told him.

"The legal troubles with my father definitely soured my opinion of the court system," Jerry said, tensing up.

"Well, reward and punishment in the afterlife are not arbitrary verdicts dished out by some scary heavenly court. Rather they should be viewed as natural consequences of our actions, both good and bad, that await us in the next world! We basically reap what we sow, and ultimately it's our own actions that become our own judges."

"I'm not sure if that is a comforting thought, exactly," Jerry said quietly. "In retrospect, some of my bright ideas don't seem so enlightened or mature."

I felt honored that Jerry was opening up, sharing his vulnerability and regrets, but I didn't want him to sink into sadness over the bitter past with his father. I decided to lighten things up with a story.

A rabbi dies, and he's waiting in line at the gates of Heaven.

Ahead of him is a guy who's dressed in sunglasses, a loud shirt, a leather jacket, and jeans. The gatekeeper angel addresses this guy, "Who are you, so that I may know whether or not to admit you to Heaven?"

The guy replies, "I'm Jack Cohen, taxi driver, from Noo Yawk City."

The angel consults his list. He smiles and says to the taxi driver, "Take this silken robe and golden staff and enter Heaven."

The taxi-driver goes into Heaven with his robe and staff, and it's now the rabbi's turn. He stands erect and booms out, "I am Joseph Snow, Rabbi of Congregation Ahavat Shalom for the last forty-three years."

The angel consults his list. He says to the rabbi, "Take this cotton robe and wooden staff and enter Heaven."

"Just a minute," says the Rabbi "That man was a taxi-driver and he gets a silken robe and golden staff. How can this be?"

"Up here, we work by results," says the Angel. "While you preached, people slept; while he drove, people prayed."

"That's a good one, Rabbi," Jerry said, chuckling. "I hope that's not a hint about how I'm handling the plane." Jerry smiled, and glanced at me for a moment.

"No, Jerry," I said. "I wouldn't have imagined how much I would enjoy flying with you. I had never been in a private plane before."

"Glad to share my favorite hobby with you," Jerry said. "For me, this is Heaven on earth. And no need to delve into guilt, perspective, or responsibility. Just the clear blue sky."

"Yes, it is true that when we arrive in Heaven we are compelled to deal with the consequential garbage we have accumulated over years of living, Jerry. That's all! Nothing more nothing less—no judges and courts, just consequences," I added. "It's nothing we can avoid, and not worth fearing."

"I don't know, Rabbi," Jerry said. "In my version of Heaven, gliding along in my plane, passing Ottawa's famous skyline on a clear day, everything is sparkling and beautiful."

"Yes, but our actions down here on earth are not random, fleeting acts that disappear like magical ink, as many would like to believe them to be," I said, glancing at Jerry. He nodded for me to continue. "On the contrary, our actions are consequential, and they set into motion a *ripple effect.* Think of it being like throwing a pebble into a lake, which sets into motion a series of ripples on the water. With our actions, we, too, set into motion ongoing *ripples,*" that eventually reach and affect the cosmos.

"Because we have set these ripples into motion, we become personally responsible for them and need to deal with them in the afterlife," I added.

"Now that's the part I don't like, Rabbi," Jerry interrupted. "I don't think it's completely fair for us to have to deal with a never-ending ripple from every single action. It's not fair."

"It's fair because we created them, Jerry. This is what is meant by 'judgment.' It is not about courtroom proceedings, but rather dealing with the good and bad forces that we have unleashed, and which are a direct consequence of our actions. They—our actions themselves—become our judges, so to speak, in Heaven."

"Well, I might have liked to know that sooner." Jerry's tone was lighthearted, but his face was serious. "So many actions are based on circumstances, and choices made in a split second. How can their effects last for eternity?"

"Jerry do you remember how I explained to you at your grandchildren's circumcisions about "garments" of the soul and how every good deed we do in this world actually creates a positive, creative angel and every misdeed creates a negative, destructive angel or demon?"

"Yes, I remember, Rabbi."

"Well, these angels and demons are the ripples. They are the consequences of our own actions. They escort us and surround us upon death. When they greet us upon our arrival in Heaven, we must deal with them for the good or the bad. We can't dismiss them or disassociate ourselves from them. They belong to us and have our stamp all over them. They literally claim us upon arrival. These angels that we have created will be our reward, and dealing with our demons will be our punishment."

"OK, Rabbi: enough of making me feel guilty for the consequences of my actions," said Jerry abruptly. "Are you ready now to bring down the plane for a landing, Rabbi? You did such a good job flying the plane that I'm sure you can figure out how to land it too."

"No Jerry," I laughed. "You must be joking?"

"I'd help you," Jerry added. "Don't worry."

I smiled to hide the terror rising in my chest. "Flying a plane is one thing but landing it and transitioning it from the air back onto the ground is another story. I will leave that to the professionals."

"Probably a wise decision, Rabbi," Jerry added.

"The way I see it, flying a plane is very much like cruising through life. While most of us become quite comfortable and proficient with the ride of life, we tend to shy away from dealing with the challenges of landing, or transitioning into the afterlife. That's where it gets tricky because we must give up the controls to a higher authority and deal with the consequences," I said, as Jerry expertly shifted the plane toward the airport.

"You keep on speaking about consequences and demons, Rabbi. Does that imply that you believe in some form of Hell in the afterlife?" Jerry asked cautiously. "Does that mean that we Jews believe in Hell as well?"

"Of course we do, Jerry."

"But Rabbi, I always thought that Jews didn't believe in Hell. I always thought that Hell was a Christian concept," Jerry said, shaking his head in surprise.

"Where do you think the other religions got the tradition of Hell in the afterlife, if not from the Jewish Bible?" I countered.

"Are you telling me that we actually believe in the fires, devils, and the pitchforks?" Jerry pressed.

"No, Jerry, not that kind of Hell! Not that kind of colorful imagery. Scenes of red devils with pointy pitchforks have captivated the imagination over the years, but they were concocted by some religious artists and writers like Dante, who viewed the afterlife strictly as an extension of their own physical existence," I said passionately.

"I've heard of Dante," Jerry said, smiling. "Rabbi, you know more than I imagined."

"These popular simplistic notions of Hell came about because the human imagination is limited to its physical experiences, which ended up distorting the true picture of Hell in the process," I explained.

"So, what is the true picture of Hell?" Jerry said in a sarcastic tone. "I always pictured Hell as my father's experience at Auschwitz. My father survived, but barely. And he was never the same, he told me."

"Your father was a true survivor. He was a walking miracle. See, Jerry, even the greatest philosophers and artists were taught by their respective religions and clergy that Hell must be some kind of physical, bodily punishment. Some even went as far as depicting hell as a massive cauldron of hot stew with potatoes, and those condemned to it were cooked in no time to a crisp."

"Like the camps," Jerry added.

"The camps were terrible. But because our soul is not physical, it can never be punished by physical means. No fire in the world is hot enough to burn or punish the spiritual soul. The physical can never hurt or affect the spiritual," I told him.

"So, if it is like you say—that Hell is not about physical suffering—then what else can it possibly be?" asked Jerry.

"Spiritual suffering." I said, scanning my brain for an example of this that Jerry might relate to. "Spiritual suffering? How can spiritual suffering have any meaningful impact if the spirit is naturally gentle, ethereal, and more than likely physically painless?"

"Think of it as the acute psychological suffering or stress that we experience in life quite regularly. Imagine Hell as the pain you experience when your granddaughter Jordana ignores your directions, or when she chooses to simply aggravate you. Or when you lose a business deal, or one of your life's dreams is unfulfilled. These emotional and psychological difficulties can be quite painful, Jerry? No?"

"Of course rejection is difficult," Jerry said.

"Because these are feelings unrelated to the body, we continue to experience this genre of profound and heartfelt pains even in a spiritual afterlife," I explained, hoping I wasn't being too vague. I felt that I should support Jerry in exploring the falling-out with his father, but I was afraid to upset him. We were still up in the air, high above the safety of earth. But I did want to make the conversation personal.

"I hear you, Rabbi," Jerry said. "But I'm not such an emotional guy. I get over lost deals and kids' antics pretty quickly."

"What about the pain a son may experience when his father stops speaking to him cold turkey? The feeling of loneliness?" I was surprised by my own boldness.

Jerry's face went white. I knew I shouldn't have brought up the sore subject of the infamous altercation between Jerry and his father. After a moment of quiet, Jerry said, "My father was devastated when I went my own way. He was so angry in the last years. I know I felt a great deal of pain. Even though he wouldn't admit it, he was hurt, too."

"So I can relate to the idea of soul-pains like trauma, strife, and agony. But what, specifically, would you say, is the particular brand of out-of-body pain that the soul experiences in Hell?" Jerry asked.

"From what I've learned, there is great untold embarrassment in store for us in the afterlife. Not only does every act we do in our lifetime have a ripple effect in the cosmos, but every moment is recorded and stored in the files in Heaven. So there is a detailed "history" of every moment of our lives, and on that day of reckoning we will be held accountable for that "history." It's no different than browsing on the computer. The computer immediately records the history of all our visits for the good and the bad. Likewise, there is a "history" button for our entire lifetime for the good and the bad, and all that we do impacts the soul by either embellishing it or tainting it. Needless to say, with everything recorded, the embarrassment can be immense," I explained.

"There are definitely some moments I'd rather forget," Jerry said. "I wish I'd known beforehand that I'd be accountable for them."

"We all have those moments, Jerry," I said, thinking of my own embarrassing and mishandled moments.

"But, Rabbi, what benefit can there possibly be in embarrassing the soul?" Jerry asked. "Who gains from this humiliating exercise?"

"The afterlife is not a matter of shaming the soul as a form of punishment and humiliation. Rather it is a case of the soul being given a new, clear perspective to the cosmos and the soul being presented with the stark truth about its life, successes and failures. Needless to say, this truth about some of our poor choices can be painful and embarrassing. That process helps the soul cleanse itself from its past blemishes, restores its purity, and generally helps it move forward in its transition," I explained.

"But Rabbi, do you really believe that up in the world of truth, there is truly a need to deal with all our mistakes and demons? Why can't we just leave them behind? What benefit can there be in punishing us with Hell, other than some divine vindictiveness or getting even? Shouldn't G–d be beyond that?" Jerry questioned.

"Hell is not about punishment. Like Heaven, it is a place where we deal with the consequences of our actions on earth. After one dies and the soul is extricated from the body, it needs to cleanse itself from the negativity of this world," I explained.

"Well, I am definitely not looking forward to the afterlife," Jerry said. "And I'm a little worried for my father, even though he was religious and tried to do the right thing in his life."

"I hear you, Jerry, but all this is for the benefit of the soul! Every evil act that we do in this world pollutes and corrupts the soul which is essentially pure. The soul cannot arrive in Heaven when it is tainted and dressed with soiled garments. For the soul to return back to its origin in Heaven, it needs to restore itself to its original pristine state: the way it was before descending down to the physical realm. This can be achieved only through an extreme cleansing process. This process is for the benefit of the soul because the soul cannot move ahead and find its place in Heaven without removing all the spiritual plaque it accumulated in this world," I said.

Jerry listened attentively as I continued.

"The Jewish mystics described this as a spiritual place called *Gehinnom*. This is usually translated as "Hell," but a better translation would be "the Supernal Washing Machine." Because that's exactly how it works. The way our soul is cleansed in Gehinnom is similar to the way our clothes are cleansed in a washing machine," I shared, hoping more details would help Jerry understand the journey of the soul.

"A washing machine, Rabbi?" Jerry sounded skeptical.

"Put yourself in your sock shoes, so to speak. If you were to be thrown into boiling hot water and flung around for half an hour, you might start to feel that someone doesn't like you. However, the fact is that it is only after going through a wash cycle that the socks can be worn again.

We don't put our socks in the washing machine to punish them. We put them through what seems like a rough and painful procedure only to make them clean and wearable again. The intense heat of the water loosens the dirt, and the force of being swirled around shakes it off completely. Far from hurting your socks, you are doing them a favor by putting them through this process," I told him.

"So what you're saying, Rabbi, is that every act we do in our lifetime leaves an imprint on our soul. The good that we do brightens and elevates our soul, and every wrongdoing leaves a stain that needs to be cleansed. If, at the end of our life, we leave this world without fixing the wrongs we have done, our soul is unable to reach its place of rest on high. We must go through a cycle of deep cleansing. Our soul is flung around at an intense spiritual heat to rid it of any residue it may have gathered, and to prepare it for entry into Heaven," Jerry said in one long exhale. "You're basically saying that Hell is soul-therapy."

"Right. It's a washing machine, not a furnace," I added.

"A washing machine?" Jerry questioned lightly.

"Yes, Jerry, to wash off all the garbage we have accumulated over the years. But let me share one more thought, Jerry, to wrap up this whole Heaven-Hell conversation and put it in perspective.

A fellow had a dream where he saw the difference between Heaven and Hell.

In Hell, he saw a huge table laden with food, in the center. Surrounding the table were starving people who all had very long forks attached to the ends of their arms. They could stab the food, but the forks were too long for them to put the food in their mouths. They were all screaming in frustration as they tried to eat the food that they longed for.

In Heaven, he saw the exact same table, laden with food, and people with the long forks at the ends of their arms. However, here, the people were all smiling and enjoying the food. What they were doing was stabbing the food and putting it into each other's mouths.

"The selfish people on earth continue being selfish in the afterlife, while the generous people continue being generous!" I summarized.

"The path we choose on earth predetermines our path in the world to come. Heaven and Hell are simply an extension of the life we choose to live down here on earth," Jerry said simply. "Basically, you make the bed you lie in!"

"Right. Heaven and Hell are not dished out based on some arbitrary court proceedings. They are consequences of our chosen path," I said. The light was fading in the late afternoon sky. My plans for the evening and my to-do list suddenly crept into my thoughts as Jerry started bringing down the plane for a landing.

"I just wonder, Rabbi: What happens to a man like my father, who suffered so much in this world? Does he at least get some credit for it?" Jerry asked, as his eyes were laser-focused on the small lights of the airport ahead. We were about to land. My heart raced as the plane smoothly drifted lower and lower. "I mean, don't Auschwitz and chemotherapy count for something toward the final score?"

Elation:

How Positivity and Resilience of the Soul Help It Deal With Suffering

I was on my way back from a meeting with the accountant for the synagogue, when I decided I needed some coffee at the local diner to help me digest the fundraising numbers. When I walked in, I saw Jerry in a heated conversation with his childhood friend, Jack Rabinowitz. I was stressed from the meeting, so I quietly made my way to the lineup for the coffee, trying not to interrupt the conversation already underway.

Jack was Jerry's childhood friend. They went to school together, graduated together, and dated together. They almost had an identical upbringing but something happened later in life that had caused them to part ways. Jack became an ardent believer, living a life according to the Torah, and Jerry became a self-proclaimed atheist.

The line was long, and I found myself eavesdropping on their conversation accidentally. I tried to refocus on the issues surrounding my synagogue building fund, but instead I overheard Jack telling Jerry, "I am sure you know that everything that happens to us is for the good. Everything must be for some reason. Nothing in this life is random, and everything that happened to your father was obviously meant to be."

"But it makes no sense, Jack. You knew my father. Morris was a good man," Jerry said. His voice was raw, and the color was rising in his neck. "He was kind. He was charitable. He was a family man. He was a great husband and father. He couldn't hurt a fly. I don't know how you feel the need to explain to me why my old man had to suffer so much. It makes absolutely no sense that he had to go through months of radiation, chemotherapy, and every other treatment under the sun. Jack paled as Jerry continued. "Do you honestly believe that my father deserved such an undignified ending? What kind of 'good,' as you say, can there possibly have been in that?"

There was an uncomfortable pause.

"I thought you told me you were getting into religion, but you sound as skeptical as ever," Jack said, disappointed.

"I've been talking with a rabbi, Jack. I'm open to listening, but I've made no commitments yet."

"I was trying to explain that G–d has a master plan for our lives, Jerry. Perhaps his suffering was to atone for some of the shenanigans of his youth, who knows? But one thing I can tell you is certain: it was not random and it was definitely meant for your father's benefit and for his own good."

Jerry's face turned red. I could see that he was getting quite agitated with Jack.

"Jack, how many years do we know each other? I believe we've known each other since we were little kids, and you knew my father very well. And he was just as you said — a very right-eous man."

"Your father was the best, Jerry," Jack said. Sensing Jerry's distress, he continued: "There was no one like your father."

"Are you saying that after all my father had gone through in the Holocaust, losing all of his family and suffering at the hands of the Nazis, that it was just not quite enough? G–d needed him to suffer just a little bit more right before he died? That is absurd. Couldn't my good father have just finished his days peacefully and pain-free? All his life he lovingly accepted his lot in life. And this is what he got in return? How could G–d have been so cruel to such a good man?" Jerry was leaning across the table toward Jack, and his voice was rising.

Other patrons in the coffee shop noticed the heated conversation. Some stared. Some looked away. But Jack wasn't fazed. He continued to stick up for G–d. He fell right into what I would describe as the 'clergy trap.'" Clergy and religious people always find it their business to become G–d's lawyer and defense team. When I first started out in the rabbinate, I remember doing exactly the same. But over the years, as I grew older and more experienced, I have learned to refrain from instinctively defending G–d, which usually backfires.

Listening to Jack, I was reminded of another story.

> An airliner flew into a violent thunderstorm and was soon swaying and bumping around the sky.
>
> One very nervous lady happened to be sitting next to a rabbi, and she turned to him. "Can't you do something?" she demanded angrily.
>
> "I'm sorry, Ma'am," the rabbi said gently. "I'm in sales, not management."

But not all clergy recognize their role as being limited to "sales," and they find the need to go the extra mile to defend G–d with some of the most inane justifications.

"No, Jerry," insisted Jack. "G–d doesn't *ever* make mistakes! There obviously must have been more to this story."

"Jack, what more could there *be* already?" Jerry said angrily. "I don't know where you're going with this, but it reminds me of why I left religion in the first place."

Jack nodded, and then continued his tirade unabashed. "Perhaps, just perhaps — even if your righteous father was not punished for his own personal sins, he still may have been punished for the other sinners of his generation! Our sages teach us that in every generation there are individual righteous people and leaders who are held responsible for the sins of the rest of their generation."

"And my father was one of them, Jack," Jerry interrupted.

"Yes, no doubt, your father was a good guy," Jack continued. "He was surely among the greats of his generation, but maybe that's ironically the very reason why he was punished. Because of the others in his generation who were not as good, he may have been held indirectly responsible for not protesting and doing enough to change their evil ways." Jack ended his speech by pounded lightly on the table, which spilled a bit of his coffee. Jerry graciously handed him a napkin.

"You see, Jerry," continued Jack, "all the people of a generation are viewed from up high as one great organic body with each part of this greater body being connected to the other. Therefore they are held responsible for each other."

"C'mon, Jack," said Jerry. "This still sounds like twisted logic — for G–d to punish the good people of the generation when He should be punishing the wicked directly. I don't get it. Why pick on the good people of a generation, when He could be punishing the sinners themselves?"

"True Jerry, but perhaps it's like an angry parent who strikes a child on the backside, although that body part never committed a sin. More than likely, it was the hands or feet of the child that misbehaved, yet it is the behind that will suffer the parent's chastisement!"

"Jack, where are you coming up with all these absurd ideas from?" Jerry said in disgust. "Who hits a child? I don't think that that is justice at all. And no one should ever have to suffer for the sins of others."

"I'm not making this up, Jerry," Jack said. "We are all responsible for each other."

"My father was, by no stretch of the imagination, a world leader, such that he should have been held responsible for his generation's wrongdoings," Jerry said judiciously.

"Jerry," continued Jack, fumbling for another explanation to defend G–d, "OK, maybe it was not for the sins of his genera-tion. But perhaps he suffered for the sins of a previous generation? You know the Bible considers time a continuum, and sometimes children need to pay for the sins of a previous generation. Perhaps he had to correct the sins of some of his not-so-perfect ancestors."

"First you go and malign my father, and now you malign his lineage too? Are you actually saying that my father had wicked grandparents and that he has to suffer for their iniqui-ties?" Jerry was enraged.

Jack watched Jerry's face redden, but he did not respond.

"This whole notion of suffering for the sins of previous generation sounds inherently wrong. Why would a benevolent and just G–d punish one generation for the sins of another?" Jerry said, with clenched teeth. He was obviously aggravated, but Jack's wheels were spinning, and he decided to respond.

"Generally speaking, that is the case" Jack agreed slowly. "But we do find circumstances where later generations need to deal with the sins of their parents. Have you ever heard of the concept of 'original sin'?"

"Is that even a Jewish concept?" Jerry asked.

"When Adam and Eve ate from the forbidden fruit in the Garden of Eden, Eve was punished with suffering painful birth pangs, Adam with making a living. The last I heard, people were still enduring these punishments until this very day. While Grandpa Adam and Grandma Eve may have long ago disap-peared from the scene, we, their descendants, still suffer for their foolishness until this very day. So there you go: children DO suffer for the sins of their parents," Jack insisted.

"This doesn't sound like the Judaism I want to have any part of," Jerry said, angrily. "It's what I left long ago, and I don't need to go back to it. You met me because you thought I was rekindling my religious practice, but honestly, this conversation is not helping my quest for comfort or truth from G–d."

There was an awkward pause. Jack didn't answer. I was standing to the side waiting for my coffee, still unseen by the sparring men.

"Listen here, Jack. I know that you are far more religious than me, but my father did send me to a good Hebrew school, and I can tell you—from the little bit that I learned there—that you are totally off base. I am pretty sure that it says, in the same Bible that you are so fond of quoting, that children shall not die for their parents' sins and each person shall die for their own sins?"

"Listen, Jerry," Jack said. "It's a possibility."

"OK. While it seems plausible that children may need to sometimes deal with their family's baggage, being punished like my father was—supposedly for the sins of his parents—sounds a bit extreme, don't you think?" said Jerry.

"All right. So maybe that's the point, Jerry!" insisted Jack. "Perhaps your father was more than just a 'descendant' of that sinful soul, but he was actually once a part of it. I learned that while children are surely not responsible for the sins of their parents, that concept applies only when they are distinct souls of their parents. But not if they share the same soul."

"Am I hearing you correctly? Are you implying that my father may have been a reincarnated soul and that he was suffering for his own sins of a previous lifetime? Are you saying that that Jews believe in reincarnation? I always thought that reincarnation was an Eastern belief that was categorically rejected by the Jews!" Jerry said, shocked. His face was flushed, and I could sense his rising tension.

Jack leaned back with the confidence of an expert as he answered Jerry. "We Jews also believe in some form of reincarnation. While we may not believe that every soul must return to earth for a second time as in some of the Eastern religions, we do believe that there may be a specific need for a soul to return. It may be to achieve a further correction of the soul, or to complete a previous mission left unfulfilled. On rare occasion, a soul must return to settle a hung jury verdict in the Heavenly court. Indeed, sometimes a soul may even return to this world simply to be cleansed here on earth, instead of having to deal with purgatory," Jack explained.

I could see that Jerry was getting sick and tired of all the complicated philosophical explanations that Jack was offering him. While Jack's arguments had some basis in Jewish tradition, reincarnation was a complex topic that needed to be dealt with sensitively. Even prominent rabbinic figures have historically approached this topic with foresight and care.

After an awkward pause, Jerry leaned forward. "First you go and malign my father and his parents, and now you go and malign all my father's previous lives," Jerry said, holding on to the table. "Does that make you feel any better? Do you feel now that you have successfully defended your G–d? Where are you going with all of this anyway? You knew my father well. He was a great man in this lifetime and you can be sure that he was a great man in his previous lifetimes too," Jerry boomed. Other diners shifted uncomfortably in their seats. Jerry glanced around the room, and then spoke quietly. "If we don't have memory of crimes committed in previous lives, what penitence or cleansing can possibly be achieved in the present life through intergenerational punishments? How can there be feelings of remorse for sins we don't ever remember committing?"

"Look here, Jerry," said Jack, changing the tone of his argument, banging his hand on the table in front of him and vibrating all the mugs filled with lukewarm coffee. "Let's face it: nobody's perfect. We all make mistakes in the course of a lifetime. Even your father, who was a righteous man, surely committed some small sins that needed correcting."

"OK, my father was human, Jack. So?" Jerry said in an angry whisper.

"So, hypothetically, your father chose to suffer with his cancer for his sins on earth in order to arrive in Heaven with a clean slate, instead of spending some time suffering in the afterlife in hell," Jack said with confidence. I wondered how to end the conversation, change the topic, anything to help Jerry escape the conversation.

"Why are you telling me this, Jack?" Jerry said with cold detachment. "You stayed religious, and I did not—in part because of the punishing nature of the ideas I learned in school. I don't know what my father would have chosen, and neither do you."

"I am not saying that we actually make this choice, Jerry," Jack continued, undeterred by Jerry's negative responses. "It would appear that these choices are made for us. But hypothetically, wouldn't we all favor a little suffering down here so that we can be spared from the ultimate suffering in the afterlife?"

"You call living through the horrors of the Holocaust 'a little suffering'? Were Buchenwald, Auschwitz, and Bergen-Belsen just 'a little suffering for a minor sin?'" Jerry said strongly. He paused for a moment before he said, "That is not justice. It is outright cruelty! What kind of small sin can possibly justify persecution and death for our people?"

"OK," conceded Jack, finally looking a little worn down. He began backtracking. "So fine, maybe we don't understand EVERYTHING. Your father was a gift to all who knew him, especially to you—even if you didn't always appreciate him," Jack said. "But life is a full package, and that's how great Jewish role models have dealt with suffering over the years."

There was a pause. Jerry didn't respond right away, and I planned a way to reveal my presence to the pair, in an effort to establish peace between them and to calm Jerry down. Before I could jump in, Jerry said, "What you're saying doesn't match with what I'm hearing from my father's rabbi."

Then Jack surprised me. "The rabbi you're speaking with is connected to Chabad *Chassidim*, right?"

Jerry nodded. "So?"

Jack continued, "I have a story told by Chabad rabbis precisely about this. Did he ever tell you this one?"

A man once came to Rabbi Dov Ber, the famed "Maggid of Mezeritch," with a question.

"The Talmud tells us," asked the man, "'a person is supposed to bless G–d for the bad just as he blesses Him for the good.' How is this humanly possible? Had our sages said that one must accept without complaint or bitterness whatever is ordained from Heaven…this I could understand. I can even accept that, ultimately, everything is for the good, and that we are to bless and thank G–d also for the seemingly negative developments in our lives. But how can a human being possibly react to what he experiences as bad in exactly the same way he responds to what he experiences as good? How can a person be as grateful for his troubles as he is for his joys?"

Rabbi Dov Ber replied, "To find an answer to your question, you must go see my disciple, Reb Zusha of Anipoli. Only he can help you in this matter."

Reb Zusha received his guest warmly and invited him to make himself at home. The visitor decided to observe Reb Zusha's conduct before posing his question. Before long, he concluded that his host truly exemplified the Talmudic dictum that puzzled him. He couldn't think of anyone who suffered more hardship in his life than Reb Zusha: there was never enough to eat in Reb Zusha's home, and his family was beset with all sorts of afflictions and illnesses. Yet Reb Zusha was always good-humored and cheerful, and he constantly expressed his gratitude to the Almighty for all His kindness.

But what was his secret? How did he do it? The visitor finally decided to pose his question.

So one day, he said to his host, "I wish to ask you something. In fact, this is the purpose of my visit to you—our Rebbe advised me that you can provide me with the answer."

"What is your question?" asked Reb Zusha.

The visitor repeated what he had asked of the Maggid. "You raise a good point," said Reb Zusha, after thinking the matter through. "But why did our Rebbe send you to me? How would I know? He should have sent you to someone who has experienced suffering!"

"Never heard that one, Jack," Jerry said, contemplating the story's connection to the discussion at hand.

"Positive people focus on what they do have, and then they are thankful for it. They never harp on what they don't have and on their suffering, Jerry," Jack said, sounding like an annoying positivity coach. I had let the conversation progress for so long now, that anything I said at this point would show I had been eavesdropping.

"I am thoroughly impressed with these exemplary rabbis, who in my humble opinion were not humans, but saints. What does that have to do with me? How can G–d expect that kind of superhuman attitude from me—or even from my father? How can He expect me to turn a blind eye to the real suffering that I personally saw my father endure? And all the more so, the pain I caused my righteous *tzaddik* of a father," Jerry said painfully. His eyes narrowed as if he were holding back tears.

I knew from my rabbinical experience that while Jack meant well with his conventional responses, and some of what he said was technically right, the timing and appropriateness of his message were totally off. No matter how awkward, it was time to jump in.

"Hi Jerry," I said, before nodding to Jack with a smile. "I was just picking up a coffee, and I admit that I overheard a bit of your discussion." Jerry looked relieved at my presence, while

Jack looked annoyed. "Rabbi, we've got to help Jerry, bring him back to the fold," Jack said with an obvious wink.

"Well, according to what I know from my mentors, it is perfectly acceptable for Jerry to question G–d," I said, hoping to diffuse the situation and change the trajectory of the conversation. I saw how Jerry's face relaxed as I was to redirect his attention away from his stubborn and unrelenting friend.

"I don't mean any disrespect, Rabbi, but isn't questioning G–d considered a form of heresy?" Jack asked.

"Judaism has a rich history of asking questions. All the greatest heroes of the Bible questioned G–d when it was necessary. They asked some really bold and daring questions," I said confidently.

"Any examples, Rabbi?" Jerry asked skeptically.

"Well, when G–d informed Abraham, the first patriarch of the Jews, that he was planning to destroy the corrupt city of Sodom, Abraham questions, "Will a just G–d kill the righteous together with the wicked?"

Jerry and Jack nodded their heads to show they were listening.

"And when G–d was about to punish the Israelites for their sin of worshipping the golden calf, Moses asks: "What will the other nations say when they find out how you punished the people you just saved?"

"I remember that one," Jerry piped in.

"And of course there's Job, the righteous man of the Bible. After being afflicted by G–d with the most immense suffering, Job asks, 'Why is it that the good people suffer and the wicked prosper?'"

"I told Jerry about the reincarnated souls, and how they are cleansed here on earth sometimes," Jack added, trying to show off his knowledge and side with me against Jerry. I didn't want to triangulate Morris's son, who needed me now more than ever.

So I continued, ignoring Jack's comment.

"These were all daring questions that could have easily been condemned by the Bible as heresies, or swept under the rug like in many other religious books and traditions," I said. "Yet, on the contrary, these arguments were openly presented as positive conversations with G–d."

Jerry squinted, and leaned back in his chair. I knew this was his listening pose, and I decided to continue.

"In fact, these biblical questions are presented and phrased so well that they are far more memorable than the answers," I pointed out. "Our tradition teaches that a good questions are far more important than the answer."

"But we aren't on the level of these biblical figures," Jack said quietly. "We don't have the right to ask questions."

"Think of Passover, when every Jewish child memorizes the famous four questions—the *Mah nishtana*—that open the proceedings of the Passover seder. While every child is familiar with the questions, I highly doubt that they even remember the answers at all. Why? Because the questions are far more important to us than the answers," I said. Jack looked aggravated, and I decided to break the tension with a joke.

An English Jew, a prominent novelist and intellectual, is informed that he will be knighted. The queen's protocol officials prepare him and other knights-to-be for the ceremony. He is informed that when he stands before the queen he is to recite certain Latin words just before being knighted.

On the day of the ceremony, the man is very nervous and, sure enough, when he approaches the queen, he forgets the Latin expression. As precious seconds tick by, the only non-English words that he remembers from the Passover seder pour out of him: *Ma nish-ta-na ha-lai-la ha-zeh mi-kol ha-lei-lot*? (Why is this night (of Passover) different than all the other nights?) The queen, confused, turns to her protocol officer and asks: "Why is this knight different from all other knights?"

Jerry and Jack both smiled, stifling a laugh at my silly pun. I decided to further lighten the mood with a story. Even though I disagreed with Jack's approach, I didn't want to alienate him—or Jerry.

> The Jewish physicist and winner of the Nobel Prize, Isidor Rabi, was once asked why he became a scientist. He replied, "My mother made me a scientist without ever intending it. Every other mother would ask her child after school, "What did you learn today?" But my mother used to ask, instead, "Izzy, did you ask a good question today?" That made the difference. Asking good questions made me into a scientist."

"Very funny, Rabbi," Jerry said with a small smile.

"Jerry, like your ancestors before you, it is perfectly alright for you to turn to G—d at this challenging moment in your life. Question the justice of the suffering of your gentle father you loved so dearly, despite your differences and rift. You are allowed to ask these tough questions. It's not heresy or apostasy. Questions are very much encouraged, Jerry," I told him as kindly as I could. Jack looked like he wanted to jump in. This exchange was tiring.

"Rabbi, with all due respect, I have read many of these biblical questions, and they are not real challenges. They are very respectful and carefully worded meek questions," Jack said with suspicion. "Jerry is too emotional now to have a true dialogue with the Creator of the Universe."

"Not true, Jack. Some of the greatest rabbis over the years have not only asked tough questions, but actually challenged G—d to bring an end to the suffering of their people," I said as confidently and calmly as I could.

"And who was that?" Jack was not letting the topic go, and needed to be right.

"Moses, for starters, was the greatest Jewish leader of all times. He went as far as demanding that G—d erase his name from the Bible, should G—d insist on bringing infliction and punishment upon the nation of Israel for worshipping the

Golden Calf. That is a powerful and unconventional challenge if I ever saw one!"

"But these great people had a relationship with G–d that is very different from what we have today. Moses saw the burning bush, and he received the Ten Commandments," Jack challenged.

"I admit Jack has a point, Rabbi," Jerry added. "I'm just a regular guy feeling distant and bitter."

"OK, let me give you a contemporary example. I witnessed this myself. This happened in the neighborhood where I grew up in Crown Heights, Brooklyn. In February, 1992, a young mother named Pesha Leah Lapine was brutally murdered. The Lubavitcher Rebbe, my mentor and the leader of world Jewry, spoke publicly about this tragedy. The Rebbe's pain was visible on his face, and he was crying as he spoke at the end of the mourning period. In his talk, the Rebbe took G–d to task over the excessive suffering of the Jewish people. I remember sitting in a sea of black-and-white-clad men listening as the Rebbe questioned G–d."

> What kind of possible divine satisfaction can there possibly be in the self-sacrifice of a mother of children? Can there possibly be a greater tragedy than a mother watching from Heaven as her children's education is given over to surrogates? What will these orphaned children gain by knowing that their mother gave up her life in sanctification of G–d's name? What will they tell their own children? Were the losses experienced in the Holocaust not quite enough? Is the suffering of 1900 years not quite enough?

Jerry and Jack shook their heads in sorrow.

"Do those heartfelt words sound meek to you, Jack?" I asked. "What do you think, Jerry?"

Jerry sighed. "The Rebbe sounds sensitive and caring. But I still don't get it. What's the point of asking good and even challenging questions if you fail to receive satisfactory answers in return? Did the Rebbe have any answers for this woman's family?"

"Herein lies one of the greatest secrets of life: there is a great benefit in verbalizing and articulating one's questions to a good listener, even if the answers are not always forthcoming," I said carefully.

"It's not easy to find good listeners," Jerry said, sounding thoughtful and worn out as he glanced quickly at Jack.

"True, we humans are so busy trying to figure ourselves out that we don't always have the patience or wisdom to truly listen to our friends, to people in pain. Yet a believer in G–d can ask hard-hitting questions, because he has an address, so to speak—somewhere to send his questions." Jerry looked askance. I continued, "True, even the believer may not get the answers, but at least he can make his case and trust that his arguments will resonate and be heard Above," I said, cautiously. Was I putting believers on a pedestal, further distancing Jerry from developing a relationship with G–d?

"What about us nonbelievers, Rabbi," Jerry said with a wink.

"Right, it's difficult to be an atheist or an agnostic. If someone truly believes that there is no rhyme or reason to anything that happens in this world, how can he ever question or protest his predicament in life?" I said, exploring Jerry's question.

"The atheist believes that everything is random and that 'that's just how the cookie crumbles,'" added Jack. "I don't understand it." Most of the other customers had left already, and we were nearly alone in the diner now. I continued on, glad we weren't preventing anyone from getting a seat or having a peaceful meal.

"I mean, life feels pretty random sometimes," Jerry countered. "It might be easier to believe the world is running on its own than to hope that there is a G–d who is somehow in charge of all that happens."

"In truth, it is only believers who can legitimately feel a sense of disappointment, betrayal, or rejection when their prayers go unanswered," I explained. "Without reasonable expectations there can never be disappointment. If you don't believe in anything at all, who exactly are you disappointed with? Disappointment comes from a subconscious expectation that there should be justice in this world. If you don't believe that there is justice, who are you angry with exactly: The monkeys? The stars? Are you angry with 'evolution'? With the 'big bang'?" I questioned, wondering where Jerry would go with my reasoning.

"I never thought about it that way," Jerry said quietly. "But is there justice? Should there be? It doesn't seem like G–d metes out reward and punishment fairly."

"With G–d at your side, you can have a meaningful dialogue about the issues of life, about the injustices you have experienced. You can rant and rave. You can pray and shout, you can demand. Ultimately you can be comforted by the thought that, at the very least, Someone who can make a difference is listening," I continued.

"How do you know G–d is listening?" Jerry asked. "Especially if He doesn't answer?"

"Well, even if you don't get a clear answer from G–d, you can always find comfort in the fact that your pain and anxiety is being shared. You are not alone in your pain. Obviously, if you are lucky and G–d answers your prayers in a manner that is satisfactory and the suffering subsides, that's great. But even if not, it is at least great to know that G–d is there feeling your pain and empathizing. He is there with you in all your challenges," I said, thinking about how I had experienced this comforting feeling at times my own life. How could I explain it?

"Isn't that a bit of a cop-out?" insisted Jerry. "Where is the comfort in knowing that someone is listening and suffering with me, if it is not accompanied with satisfactory tangible results?

And if there is no answer, why not just unload to a friend?"

Jack stretched his arms back, as if his whole body was yawning. This never-ending discussion was exhausting for all of us. I wondered what I could say to answer this unanswerable question.

I continued doggedly, hoping a story might help address the issue. "I hear your frustration. There's a story from the Holocaust that I think will help us sort through this age-old dilemma. It's a story that has been told on many occasions by the famous Holocaust survivor and scholar, Elie Wiesel, who witnessed this story himself."

> A group of inmates convened a court case in a bunker in Auschwitz, bringing G–d Almighty Himself to trial. With no options left for these broken souls during the Holocaust, what were they to do?

Jerry shrugged his shoulders. I wondered if he could picture his father in his mind's eye, struggling in the camps.

> The inmates made elaborate and thorough presentations representing both the defense and the prosecution in front of the judges, who were chosen from among themselves. Most of the participants had past experience in the judiciary field. After carefully hearing both sides of the case, and after much serious deliberation, the judges of the ad hoc court presented their astounding ruling.
>
> The makeshift court found G–d guilty for breach of contract with the Jewish people, whom he had promised never to forsake, and for crimes committed against humanity. Then, in a moment of complete irony, after presenting their ostensibly heretical verdict, the judge stood up, banged on the table, and invited the prosecution, the defense, and the rest of the inmates present to pray the daily afternoon service.

"That story reminds me of my father," Jerry said, suddenly sounding excited. "He was profoundly angry at G–d, yet would not miss even one of his daily prayers as long as he was able to walk."

I chuckled, envisioning Morris handing out candy to the kids, bringing so much life and excitement to our little synagogue. He showed up every day, despite his pain and anger.

"I inherited the animosity but not the religious fervor," said Jerry wryly.

"Now tell me: How in the world were these broken and tortured Holocaust survivors capable of prayer after all they endured?" I said, ignoring Jerry's comment about his own struggle with faith. "How was a service in Auschwitz possible at all after these inmates themselves had just handed down a guilty verdict against G–d? Where did they find any space in their hearts for any prayer after expressing their protest? Were their prayers a capitulation to G–d, or a display of superhuman faith? Were they putting their heads in the sand, or was there, maybe, some great, deeper wisdom in their paradoxical behavior?" I wondered aloud.

"*Nu*, Rabbi...what's the answer?" Jerry asked. Jack sat, quietly defeated, but listening.

"The answer is that what these prisoners did is precisely the Jewish way. Shout all you want, and question everything, but never reject the Author of life," I said with conviction.

"Even if he rejected you?" Jerry said, unconvinced.

"Yes, that's the trick, Jerry," I said, "to come back and pray to your Creator, who is the true lifelong companion, even if you feel at times like you have been ignored by Him. Even if your prayers seem categorically rejected, or just plain unanswered, continue to pray, because in the long run, the loneliness of not having a caring and listening ear is even more painful."

"While these concentration camp inmates exercised their basic right to a fair day in court, shouting out at the heavens, making their case and even disagreeing with their lot in life, they simultaneously accepted the fact that there was a higher force at play in this world and chose to submit themselves to it and continued to pray to it and embrace it," I said passionately.

"They were amazing," Jack and Jerry said in unison.

"It's definitely not a perfect situation. Suffering and pain is never a good thing, Jerry. But at least when you know that you have company in your suffering, a listening ear at your side, it is that much more bearable."

Jerry nodded. Jack smiled.

"It says in the Bible, in the book of Isaiah, chapter 63, verse 9, "In all their suffering, He suffered," I quoted.

"Jerry, I am sure you know this famous story," I continued.

> A man dreamed he was walking with G–d. Across the sky flashed scenes of his life. And for each scene, he noticed two sets of footprints in the sand: one belonged to him, and the other to G–d.
>
> And when the last scene of his life flashed before him, he again looked back at the footprints in the sand. He noticed that many times along the path of his life there was only one set of footprints…. He also noticed that it had happened at the very lowest and saddest times in his life, at times when he was about to give up all hope.
>
> This really bothered the man and he questioned G–d about it. "G–d, You said that once I decided to follow You, You'd walk with me all the way. But I have noticed that during the most troublesome times in my life, there is only one set of footprints. I don't understand why, when I needed You most, You would leave me."
>
> G–d replied, "My precious child, I love you, and I would never leave you. During your times of trial and suffering, when you see only one set of footprints, it was then that I carried you."

I was not sure whether I had convinced Jerry with my subtle philosophical point about divine companionship, so I decided there and then to take a head-on personal approach with Jerry.

"Jerry it's time you realize how much you resemble your father," I blurted out.

"What do you mean by that, Rabbi?" asked Jerry, surprised. "Everyone says I'm like my mother."

"Well, it is quite obvious to anyone who has ever met you and your father, that the two of you look alike," I said, picturing Morris in my mind. Jerry was the spitting image of his father. "You walk like him and talk like him. You even do business like him. You are your father in so many ways," I said in earnest. "I believe, Jerry, that it's time that you emulated his approach to dealing with life's tragedies as well. Becoming more like your father will help you deal with your own personal loss, and it will help you cope with some of the depressing and obsessive thoughts about your father's inexplicable suffering." I locked eyes with Jerry, so he could feel the warmth and care I felt for him.

"So, what is this approach that you are attributing to my father?" Jerry asked, turning away from my strong stare.

"Look at your father and his friends — that resilient and courageous group we all look up to for being Holocaust survivors," I said. "Your father had a choice. He could have followed the group of 'rejectionists' — those survivors who, after experiencing the atrocities of the Holocaust, felt abandoned, and rejected their faith in G–d and humanity."

Jerry nodded. "I relate to that approach."

"Then, there was a second group who, instead of giving up their faith, became stronger, more passionate believers, embracing G–d and religion even more than before the war," I said. "In my view, both groups are valiant heroes of the Holocaust era simply for what they'd had to live through."

"That rings true," Jerry said. "My parents had very different reactions to the atrocities they experienced in the camps. And both views seemed justified to me."

"Your father was clearly from the group of survivors who was visibly proud of his faith. Jerry you can follow in your father's ways. You need to embrace your faith," I said, stepping over the line, giving unwanted advice. Jerry was silent.

"Your father's approach reminds me of Victor Frankl, the famous Viennese psychologist who lived through the horrors of the Holocaust himself. Frankl developed a unique system of psychology, based on his own experiences in the death camps, that he called *logotherapy*. Indeed, over the years, many people dealing with terminal illness and other major challenges in life have found his writings very helpful and therapeutic."

Jack piped in, "My wife read Frankl's book."

"One of the major ideas Frankl discusses is that even if we cannot choose the nature of the challenges life presents, we can choose how to react to them. We can either view ourselves as fighting "victors" or hapless "victims." We have the choice. We can either feel sorry for ourselves and throw in the towel, or we can apply positive thinking and focus on a purpose in life and live to fight another victorious day," I explained.

"Jerry, your father was clearly the 'victor' type if I've ever met one," I said again, hoping Jerry could hear me. "And you can follow in his footsteps, just like you do in so many areas."

"But Rabbi, maybe by blindly holding on to his old faith, my father failed to learn the practical lessons of the Holocaust while those that rejected their faith were right?" Jerry said.

"It's not a question of right and wrong here. It's simply a question of how we react to the challenges we are presented. The issue is whether we choose to maintain a positive perspective on life, reaffirming our reason to live and our purpose for existence, or whether we give up on ourselves. There are always two ways of looking at anything in this world. The cup half-full or half-empty. Even with an experience as devastating and debilitating as the Holocaust, there are always two ways to react," I said, thinking how I might apply this approach myself.

"That's all you've got, Rabbi?" Jack said, challenging me. "Cup half-full or half-empty?"

"Well, the famous Nazi-hunter Simon Wiesenthal once told a very insightful story about interpreting the facts with a 'positive perspective' that he claims changed his own view on life," I answered. I cleared my throat and then launched into the story:

> It was in Mauthausen, shortly after the war ended and the concentration camps were liberated. Rabbi Eliezer Silver, head of the Union of Orthodox Rabbis of North America, came to the camp on a mission to offer aid and comfort to the survivors. Rabbi Silver also organized a special service, and he invited Wiesenthal to join the other survivors in prayer.
>
> Mr. Wiesenthal declined, explaining why: "In the camp," Mr. Wiesenthal said to the rabbi, "there was one religious man who had somehow managed to smuggle in a *siddur* [prayer book].
>
> "At first, I greatly admired the man for his courage—that he'd risked his life in order to bring the siddur in. But the next day I realized that, to my horror, this man was 'renting out' this siddur to people in exchange for food. People were giving him their last piece of bread for a few minutes with the prayer book. This man basically made a business out of religion. What a disgrace!" Wiesenthal continued: "If this is how religious Jews behave, I'm not going to have anything to do with a prayer book."
>
> He turned to walk away, when Rabbi Silver touched him on the shoulder and gently said in Yiddish, "Why do you choose to look at the Jew who used his siddur to take food out of starving people's mouths? Why don't you look at the many Jews who gave up their last piece of bread in order to be able to use a siddur?"
>
> This point left an amazing impression on me and was a turning point in my life," said Wiesenthal.

"I get your point, Rabbi," Jerry said, nodding his head toward Jack.

"What a perspective shift," Jack added.

"We can either focus on the scoundrels of this world, whose inconsiderate and selfish crimes make us question our faith, or we can choose to focus on the good guys of this world, whose selfless and noble actions will strengthen our faith," I explained.

"What you're saying, Rabbi, is that an identical life experience can either make us a cynic or a believer," Jerry clarified. "It all depends on how we choose to look at things."

"This applies to both the way we view our fellow man, and the way we view our G–d as well," I said. "Your father was a positive man, Jerry, and he made a conscious choice to look at life in a positive light."

"I hear you, Rabbi, but I need to know for myself from where, from what place inside of himself, could my father have possibly mustered optimism in such a dark world? How did he manage to view his life with over-the-top positivity, when doom and gloom should have dictated his disposition after the Holocaust?" Jerry paused, and he took a deep breath before continuing. "Rabbi, if I had been placed in his position, I would have certainly thrown in the towel. My father's reaction seems unnatural."

"I know that it may sound counterintuitive, but it is optimism, not pessimism, that is natural to the human condition, and it comes from our soul," I said, words pouring from my heart. "From our divine spark, the very essence of our being. That's where optimism and positive energy flow from."

"Not everyone seems to have this positivity, Rabbi," Jerry said, sounding skeptical.

"Just like the soul and its personality are indestructible, so too this intrinsic positive energy that flows from the pure essence of the soul cannot be destroyed," I explained. "This constant river of optimism emanating from the soul gives us the ability to reboot, even after encountering the most ugly and depleting life experiences. In fact, this force is so powerful that the more we suppress it, the stronger it becomes."

"If you're talking about my father, you're right, Rabbi," Jerry said with a small smile that looked just like Morris's. "But this soul force you speak of seems inaccessible to me."

"Your father chose to align himself with that unstoppable, indefatigable soul that's really within each of us," I said. "He was able to tap into its happiness and positivity. I saw this firsthand, and so did you over the years."

"I could never understand it," Jerry said with emotion. "I felt like I had to be angry about the Holocaust for him."

"Now it's time for you, Jerry Goldstein, to step up to the plate, and take over where your father left off by emulating his healthy, optimistic approach to life. Why don't you tap into your own natural reservoir of optimism?" I prodded.

"Rabbi, I just don't have it in me," Jerry said quietly.

"Maybe it's time for yet another story," Jack said, giving Jerry space to collect himself. Both men sat attentively as I began.

Rabbi Nissen Mangel of New York was once rushing down Orchard Street on the Lower East Side of Manhattan on a Friday afternoon, to make it home for the Jewish Sabbath.

An old man who was sitting on a bench in front of his store and selling discounted shirts displayed on the street, stopped him.

"What's the rush, young man? Come in and buy some discounted shirts! These are bargains you don't want to miss!"

"It's almost the Sabbath, and I must catch the bus home," answered the panting rabbi.

"For the Sabbath you are willing to forgo such incredible bargains?"

"Yes, of course. To me, the Sabbath is very important."

"Sabbath?" said the old man. "I used to do that when I was a child in Europe, but not anymore."

"Why's that?" asked the Rabbi.

The old man's face turned very serious. He pounded his chest and said, "Young man, I was in Auschwitz, and if you saw what I saw and experienced what I experienced, you would never believe in G–d or keep the Sabbath!"

The Rabbi froze in his tracks, very moved by the older man's remarks. But he did not miss a beat. Catching the old man totally by surprise, he rolled up his sleeve, pointed to the tattooed number on his arm, and responded, "I, too, am a survivor of Auschwitz, and I still keep the Sabbath. After G–d miraculously spared me, a nine -year-old boy in Auschwitz, how could I not keep the Sabbath?"

"Have a Good Sabbath," said the Rabbi to the surprised old man, and off he went to catch his bus.

"A Good Sabbath to you, too," muttered the old man, deep in thought.

Rabbi Mangel lives today in Brooklyn, New York and is the father of many children, a number of whom became rabbis. "I guess it all depends on how you look at things," Jack added. "Same experience, different understanding."

"Jerry, over the years I had many personal conversations with your father," I said, treading carefully around the topic of my close bond with Morris, versus Jerry's fraught ties. Today Jerry seemed relaxed, and he nodded warmly, validating my bond with his dad. I continued, "Despite all of Morris's questions about where G–d was during the Holocaust, and the injustices he personally experienced, he always kept his faith and maintained a positive attitude, bringing candy to synagogue for the kids, and making jokes. I would often ask him, 'Morris, how do you deal with all the ugly memories of the war?'

"I never thought to ask him that," Jerry said, breaking out of his reverie. "I'm so curious. What did he say?"

"He would answer in Yiddish, *Men darf nit trachten; min darf tohn*—which roughly translates as 'One need not think; one needs to do,' I told him.

"That was his way," Jerry agreed.

"Were your father and his friends in denial of their traumatic past? Definitely not. He and his friends made a conscious choice to tap into the natural positivity emanating from their souls to redirect their lives in an upbeat, positive direction," I added.

"I never thought of it that way," Jerry said. "I just wanted him to be real, to understand my angst, and not be so perfectly content. I felt like there was no room for my juvenile suffering. How could I get upset over anything, when my father had gone through so much, and was so strong and positive?"

"It's tough, Jerry," I said, feeling connected to him, and connected to his struggles. "Our parents' generation went through so much."

Jerry didn't answer right away. He looked pensive. Finally, Jack broke the awkward silence. "You got another story, Rabbi? This is heavy stuff. We can all use a story!"

I smiled. "You bet."

Did you hear that it was announced in Tel Aviv that G–d was going to send a tidal wave, thirty feet high, over the city because of its sins?

"Uh, no, Rabbi," Jack answered skeptically. "I never heard of that."

Well, hearing of the tidal wave, Muslims went to their mosques to pray for a speedy progression to the paradise of their prophet. Christians went to their churches to pray for the intercession of the saints. The Jews went to the synagogues and prayed, "Oh G–d, teach us how to live under 30 feet of water!"

"Oh Rabbi, that's a good one," Jack said, chuckling.

"We're laughing now, but this is how these incredible survivors dealt with their lives after the destruction of the Holocaust. These timeless heroes believed that there was a greater purpose in life, and they would find a way to get it back, even after being derailed and sidetracked. They were visionaries who were on a mission to perfect the world. Yes, they understood very well what had happened, and were extremely disappointed that their life mission had been sidetracked by extremely painful challenges. But that is exactly what their hardships were: challenges to face and overcome," I explained.

"The Holocaust was more than a challenge," Jack said sharply.

"The point is that even after Morris and many of his peers experienced the atrocities of the Holocaust, they were not paralyzed. They were not busy working out whether they deserved it or not. Instead, they immediately got busy with getting their life mission back on track. Like the Jews in Auschwitz, who, even after finding G–d guilty for not being fair to them, from their limited human perspective, immediately returned to praying the afternoon prayer service, your father and his friends knew they had a job to get done. They got back to changing the world, without harping onto their tragedy and loss, which was impossible to understand."

"I seem to be more paralyzed over the loss of my father than he was from all his suffering through the war and illnesses," Jerry noticed.

"Your father was a very wise man. Hold on to his world vision, Jerry. Hold on to your father's coattails, and you will be just fine. I guarantee that you will overcome this setback."

"I feel that I'm getting my first glimpse into my father's worldview. I had always blocked it out, wanting to pave my own way in the world," Jerry said. His voice was heavy with emotion. "I didn't appreciate how great he was—what he gave me."

Jack sat there, motionless, his eyes glistening from held-back tears.

"One last story, and then I think we need to go, or at least order more coffee," I said, glancing at my watch.

Both Jerry and Jack shook their heads in agreement, searching for a waiter who would bring us the check.

I continued, "There is a moving story from the Holocaust, told about the great Bluzhever Rebbe."

One night, the German guards came into his bunk and ordered everyone up and out. They were to march to a field where a pit had been dug — deep and wide. "Everyone must try to jump across," shouted the guard. "If you miss, you're dead."

The Jews were hungry and weak. It was pitch dark and cold. One at a time the Jews tried but hardly anyone made it.

Standing next to the Bluzhever Rebbe in line was another Jew. He said to the Rebbe, "We'll never make it across. So, rather than entertaining the guards, let's just sit down right here and let them shoot us."

"No," replied the Rebbe. "We must try."

Within moments, it was their turn in line. They jumped together and both made it safely to the other side.

Stunned, the other Jew turned to the Rebbe and asked: "You're an old man! How did you do it?"

Explained the Rebbe, "As I got ready to jump, I thought of my father and grandfather and of our great and holy sages from generations past. I thought of Maimonides and Rashi. I thought of Moses and King David. I thought of Sarah and Rachel. As I jumped, I held onto their coattails. It was they who pulled me across."

"But," the Rebbe asked the man, "How did you do it?"

"Oh, me? I was holding on to your coattails."

"Hold on to your father's coattails, Jerry!" I said with emotion.

"We all should try and emulate your dad, Jerry," added Jack.

Jerry grinned. We all got up from our chairs, patting each other on the back as we paid the check. As we headed for the door, I could picture Morris smiling at us from Heaven.

CONVERSATION 5

Connection:
How Can We Reconnect With the Soul After Death?

A few quiet weeks went by. I was focused on my new strategy for salvaging my synagogue. Plans for renovations were being finalized, even though I wasn't yet sure how to pay for them, or if my small congregation would survive to enjoy them. I was brainstorming some new class ideas when Jerry called. He told me, through sobs, that he was at the cemetery.

"Rabbi, I need your help. I am standing beside my father's grave, and I feel completely lost. I need somehow to reconnect and speak to my father again, to rectify our broken relationship. I need to make amends with him. Rabbi, can you please come over and help me? I need to know what to do."

While I was very familiar with Jerry's chronic guilt, it still came to me as a surprise that the strong-headed superstar entrepreneur would show me such vulnerability. It wasn't like Jerry to bare his soul like that.

"Of course, Jerry, I am on my way!" I assured him as I ran out the door to meet with him to help.

I quickly made my way to the cemetery. It was a scene out of the movies. It was a grey day, and Jerry's mood reflected the gloominess. I saw it in his eyes. There he was, a successful millionaire sitting stooped on the floor right near his father's grave, looking tragically lost between the headstones.

"Rabbi, I am glad you could make it over." Jerry looked up at me, failing to make direct eye contact. He looked like a wreck.

"I have an important question bothering me that I need to ask you," he said, sounding tired.

"Sure, Jerry. Anything. How can I help you?" I truly wondered how he would manage to communicate with me in such a broken state, but then he sat up straight, looked me straight in the eye, and began speaking.

"OK, Rabbi. Assuming that there actually is a Heaven like you've been telling me all along, and assuming that my father, being the good man that he was, has peacefully transitioned and settled there, is it then still possible for me to make a meaningful connection with him? Is there a way for me to communicate with him in Heaven from this remote planet earth? Rabbi, I don't know why, but standing here at the graveyard, I am overtaken by a sense of hopelessness. I feel that my dad is so far away that there is no way for me to ever reconnect with him." Jerry sighed and his shoulders shook.

"But, on the other hand, I must admit," he continued, "I have another part of me that seems to be drawing me closer to my father. Honestly, I only came here today because I was mystically drawn here. Something deep down inside me said that there must be some way to connect to my father, here in the cemetery."

"Jerry, your gut feeling is right. Living in this modern age of worldwide communications helps us envision how we can find a meaningful connection to Heaven too. Especially someone like you, who successfully built your own business in the communications industry. The cornerstone of your business is the principle that we can connect everywhere."

"Business communication is one thing, but communicating with my father was difficult even when he was alive," Jerry said. "Now that he's gone, I feel desperate to reconnect. Yet with all my experience in communications, I don't feel knowledgeable on how to reach him now, even if, as you say, it is possible."

"It *is* possible. There are a number of spiritual channels to

Heaven that I have learned about in the mystical books of the Kabbalah. They are like portals on the computer," I explained.

"Hmm, sounds interesting. Tell me more," Jerry said.

"The first 'portal' through which you can make a meaningful connection to the soul of your dear father is right here, as you suspected, at the cemetery. By visiting the cemetery plot, you can make a very meaningful connection. The soul of the deceased is present here, very much so; it hovers over its former body and continues to maintain a connection with the space of the grave, even posthumously. When we visit the grave we can reconnect to the soul," I told him.

"C'mon Rabbi," said Jerry. "This sounds to me like some hocus pocus voodoo worship. Assuming that my father is in a spiritual world now, what difference does it make where his dysfunctional physical remains are buried? What difference does it make to him if I am standing praying at his grave, or speaking to him while sipping coffee in Starbucks? If he's truly a spirit, and not constrained by time or space, shouldn't I be able to connect with him anywhere?"

"Well, did you ever hear the story about phone calls to G–d?" I asked. Jerry shook his head *no* and motioned for me to continue with my "rabbinical" story.

"Here goes," I said, launching into a lighthearted tale.

An influential American preacher went to see the pope in Rome. While he was waiting, he noticed a red phone. As he was ushered in to talk to the pope, he asked, "What's the red phone for?"

"That's to talk to G–d," came the reply.

"Really?" the reverend gasped. "How much does such a call cost? It's an awfully long way!"

"$10,000 a minute, but it's well worth it," answered the pope.

Some weeks later, the preacher went to see the chief rabbi in Jerusalem. He noticed that he, too, had a red phone. "I don't suppose," asked the reverend, "that this phone is to talk to G–d?"

"Yes it is," came the reply.

"And how much does that cost?" the preacher inquired.

"Twenty cents a minute," shrugged the chief rabbi.

"How come it's so cheap?" the American asked. "The pope has a phone like that and it costs $10,000 a minute!"

"Well," grinned the chief rabbi, "From here it's just a local call."

"Well, we're not in Jerusalem," Jerry said. "What's the point?"

"Truth be told, Jerry, there are ways to connect to your father from just about anywhere in this world, even from a Starbucks. But then there are some special places, where making a connection is easy, like making a "local call." Knowing those places can be extremely useful in making an easy, fast connection," I ventured.

Jerry motioned for me to continue, as we stared at his father's headstone.

"To use a modern-day example: while there is, theoretically, internet service available everywhere, it is best to find a portal or Wi-Fi hot spot to gain accessibility and make the desired connection," I said, hoping he would relate to this example. "So, the first hotspot in this world is the burial place of the body; in other words, the grave."

"Rabbi, if that's the case, why don't I feel anything here? To be frank, all I am feeling here is that there is a dead body in a box with a tombstone sitting over it. There are no traceable signs of life to be found in this entire cemetery anywhere," Jerry said mournfully.

"But Jerry," I responded quietly, "you did share that you felt something. Why else would you have come running here first thing in the morning, when you felt down and wanted to reach out to your father? Obviously, somewhere deep down inside your own soul this place resonates with you, and you believed that you could make a meaningful connection here."

"Maybe I was overtired," Jerry said sadly. "I was confused after a sleepless night."

"Well, maybe you sensed that the grave is a really powerful place and a natural portal to the soul. It is the place where we can experience how the symbiotic relationship between body and the soul—a connection that began at birth and then continued an entire lifetime—logically carries over into the posthumous state. It makes sense that, after an entire lifetime of the body serving as the faithful vessel of the soul, it should continue that role in some way even after death," I told him, as he shifted his gaze toward the grave again.

"Maybe. I just can't sense it. It seems that the body's job is over now," he said, shaking his head.

"Jerry, the physical body can be compared to the original Hebrew 'Temple' in Jerusalem that, according to the Bible, was the physical vessel for G-d in this world and was the universal channel through which to connect with Him. Yet, despite the destruction of the physical Temple in the year 70 C.E., the place of its remaining ruins is still considered the most important place for Jews to pray until this very day. On any given day, there are thousands of Jews and other people praying at the Western Wall, the last remaining vestige of the original Temple."

"OK, the Wall is special. It's my first stop whenever I visit Israel," Jerry conceded. "But what's the connection between ruins in Israel, and a cemetery outside of Ottawa?"

"Likewise, the remains of the body, which served as the physical "temple" and home for the soul, although it may have disintegrated after death, remains a potent channel through which to reach the soul in Heaven," I continued.

"Rabbi, do you mean to say that there is actual life at the grave?" Jerry questioned.

"Yes, well, sort of…but not exactly, Jerry. The grave is a like a "channel" to the soul in Heaven. The Kabbalah takes it a step further and maintains that there is some form of life—a lower level of the soul that remains in a ghostlike form at the actual gravesite—but the general consensus of Jewish thinkers is that the gravesite is only a portal. But it's a powerful one." I explained this esoteric topic as best I could.

"This sounds like science fiction," Jerry said.

"Because the body is an essential portal to the soul, Judaism and many other respected religions strongly oppose the practice of cremation. The decision to cremate the body robs family and friends access to the soul of their departed loved one," I told him. I was grateful that Jerry had followed Morris's burial instructions, and left the body intact.

"But, Rabbi, how can the body serve as a portal if it eventually disintegrates anyway? With nothing left, what kind of channel can it serve, if it no longer exists?" Jerry wondered.

"The Talmud maintains that, even many years after death, there are some remains of the body left at the grave. According to tradition, there is a small bone on top of the spine, known as the *luz* bone, which never disintegrates. It is indestructible. It is from this bone that, tradition says, the resurrection of the dead will begin one day."

"Whoa, Rabbi, that's wild," Jerry interjected. "Jews believe in resurrection of the dead?"

"The Talmud tells the story that when the Roman Emperor Hadrian, of the first century, heard about the indestructible *luz* bone from the rabbis, he obtained one and tried to grind it, burn it, and dissolve it in water, to no avail. When he hammered it against an anvil, the hammer and anvil broke," I shared.

"That's weird, Rabbi," Jerry commented.

"Yes, yet this indestructible bone is the physical counterpart of its symbiotic partner, the indestructible soul," I said.

"It's hard to imagine a bone that is so strong," Jerry noted.

"Well, this *luz* bone that we are discussing is very much

like the Western Wall, the sole remaining indestructible wall, the last surviving part of the original Temple. The Temple, as we discussed before, was the geographic equivalent of the human body," I said, hoping my examples were clear.

"Right," Jerry said.

"Just as the Temple housed the presence of G–d in this world, the human body houses the spark of G–d—the soul," I continued. "And just as the Temple was never completely destroyed by our enemies—because the Western Wall always remained—the human body, too, never completely disintegrates because a little *luz* bone always remains."

Jerry nodded, urging me on.

"And the good news is that, just as we are taught that the Western Wall will serve as the kernel from which the rest of the future Temple will be rebuilt, so, too, the human body will be reconstructed from the *luz* bone in the time of the resurrection of the dead," I finished, curious about what Jerry's reaction would be.

"Wow!" said Jerry. "That is really interesting. It always bothered me how there was supposed to be a resurrection of the dead when we know that the body eventually disintegrates and is gone."

"Yes, and this explanation also gives us a scientific explanation of how resurrection works altogether. You see, up until recently, the belief in the resurrection of the dead was totally dismissed by the scientific community as archaic dogma that Judaism and other religions have held for thousands of years. Resurrection of the dead has been subjected to ridicule and comedy. Even many religious scholars have been forced to reinterpret resurrection as some symbolic renewal of spirit and hope. They were literally so embarrassed by this seemingly "science fiction" belief, that they rejected its simplistic meaning and created allegorical interpretations of it," I went on.

"I'm tempted to agree with those allegorical interpretations, Rabbi," Jerry said. "Resurrection is a pretty outrageous concept. Look, we are surrounded by decaying, silent bodies out here."

"It is hard to relate to, Jerry. Yet, with recent scientific progress in the field of DNA research and cloning, it has been shown that just one small strand of the original DNA is able to reproduce an identical body even thousands of years later. But to accomplish this feat, we will first need to find this remnant of DNA. So, how do we find it?"

"Sounds difficult," Jerry commented.

"The answer is the *luz* bone. Yes, that indestructible bone, that never disintegrates or decomposes, offers a plausible scientific explanation to the seemingly mythical tradition of resurrection," I told Jerry.

"It does seem like a myth," Jerry added. "And I usually think of Judaism as practical, rather than magical."

"Jerry, I must make a confession. Up until recently, I myself wondered why it would be necessary for the all-powerful Creator to reconstruct the body from the miniscule luz bone," I shared. "If, at the end of the day, we are relying on a miracle to reconstruct the body, why not do it from scratch?"

"I hear what you're saying, Rabbi," Jerry added. "Why does this bone matter so much?"

"With recent scientific advancement in the area of cloning, resurrection is no longer some hocus pocus, magical feat. It is possible within natural means. This one little bone is responsible for the resurrection of the human body," I said.

"What does this have to do with visiting the grave, Rabbi?" Jerry asked, bringing us back to the present moment: a grey day in the cemetery.

"The *luz* bone remains forever at the grave, both to facilitate the revival of the dead in the future and to serve as a powerful prayer portal to the soul in Heaven. Because of the *luz* bone, we can successfully communicate with our loved ones at the grave," I explained.

"Hold on," interrupted Jerry, "Didn't I learn, many years ago in Hebrew school, that we Jews don't believe in speaking to the dead? Don't we believe that praying to the dead is akin to an idolatrous practice? Doesn't relying on the dead diminish our faith in G–d?" Jerry's questions were bubbling out of him all at once. He paused for a moment, and then his questions continued. "Rabbi, correct me if I'm wrong. From my limited understanding, praying through any intermediary, even if it is an elevated spirit, is forbidden! So how do you reconcile these elementary Jewish beliefs with praying at a gravesite?"

"Jerry you are one hundred percent right," I said. "Of course we don't pray to the dead. The dead don't have any autonomous powers to help us. We only pray to G–d himself. But, in order that our prayers should reach up to the heavens, we need, as we discussed before, to tap into the proper channel and portal," I told him. This was a nuanced topic, and I hoped I could clarify it for Jerry.

Jerry nodded, shifting his feet.

"It's like choosing to pray at a synagogue building, as opposed to praying privately at one's home. While G–d is everywhere, we give preference to a public house of prayer, because praying in a synagogue has more of a powerful and impactful connection on high. Likewise with the cemetery, the holy ground where the righteous person is buried which, like a synagogue, is much more effective when the prayers are offered at this sacred space. Furthermore, special consideration is given to our prayers when submitted at the grave in the merit of the good deeds of our loved ones who are buried there. Their merits make our prayers even more potent and favorable," I said, hoping to offer solace to Jerry.

"Thanks, Rabbi, but didn't you tell me that at the cemetery

I will be communicating with my dad directly, and not just cashing in on his merits to grant me a personal audience with G–d?"

"Yes, don't worry, Jerry. You can speak directly to your father at his grave. The masters of the Kabbalah write that, although we generally pray to G–d alone and are not allowed to pray to or summon the spirits, we do have permission to ask the deceased to "advocate" on our behalf. Obviously, the most eligible candidates for this mammoth task are our loved ones, who, throughout their lifetime, tirelessly advocated on our behalf, and by extension, should continue doing so posthumously with the same dedication and gusto as before," I said with conviction.

"I think I get it," Jerry said thoughtfully. "Can you just clarify the last bit, Rabbi?"

"Sure, of course, Jerry. So, when we are visiting the grave of a loved one, while we don't actually pray "to" them or attribute any divine powers to them, we can ask them to kindly intercede on our behalf, and to advocate our cause up high. They are the best we've got," I said emphatically. I pictured Morris reaching his arms toward Jerry, embracing him in a heavenly hug.

Jerry swayed as I spoke, lost in his own reverie. I decided to fill the quiet by continuing to explain how departed souls help their loved ones.

"In Yiddish, this process of heavenly advocacy is called being a "*gutte better*—a good advocate," I explained.

"I always wondered what that phrase meant," Jerry added. "And why people were wishing the departed should get "better." Jerry chuckled at the double meaning of the word "better."

"Indeed, it is customary to comfort a mourner with this term. Saying 'May your loved one become *a gutte better*' is basically a heartfelt wish that the loved one they are mourning should stand up and advocate their case at the heavenly tribunal," I continued, hoping this made things clearer.

"But, Rabbi, this is assuming your loved one wants to advocate," Jerry said, turning his head away from me, toward his father's grave.

"What do you mean by that, Jerry?" I sensed Jerry's pain, but wasn't sure how to direct the conversation.

"Well, Rabbi, what if you were not on good terms with the deceased? Would he advocate on your behalf regardless?" Jerry said, in a choked voice. I waited while he regained composure. "To be more specific, you know very well about the strained relationship I had with my father over the last few years.

Jerry was, of course, referring to the unfortunate time when his father had abruptly cut off all contact with Jerry.

"Do you really think I can still look forward to my father advocating for his disenfranchised, disowned son?"

"Jerry, I can't really answer that question," I said, feeling bad for him. "To be totally honest, I do believe like I have told you before, that Morris is in a world of truth, and more than likely regrets his overreacting to your behavior. But then again, I can't speak for him. It is still possible that he carries some grievances. All I can recommend to you is that you ask your father for forgiveness, Jerry," I said tentatively. I felt awkward and out of my depth. How would I both comfort Jerry *and* help him work through his strained relationship with Morris?

"Forgiveness? Rabbi, you have got to be kidding. My father is dead! Don't you see that it's too late for forgiveness?" Jerry said in an aggravated tone.

"There are still ways to achieve forgiveness, even posthumously, by praying at this grave and opening up your heart to him," I said, staying calm.

"How does that work, Rabbi?" Jerry said cynically.

I decided to take a chance and tell Jerry about the unusual mystical ritual to achieve posthumous forgiveness:

"There is a mystical tradition that, in order to successfully solicit forgiveness from a deceased loved one, one needs to bring another nine men to the cemetery to make a quorum of ten and then publicly ask for forgiveness from the deceased relative in front of the group," I shared.

"That sounds embarrassing," Jerry said quietly. "Why must there be a quorum?"

"The mystics speak about the mystical power of the quorum, and how asking for forgiveness at the cemetery in their presence increases one's chances to receive the forgiveness requested. The quorum has the power of synergy to pierce the heavens, elicit higher levels of divine compassion, and, ultimately, draw down forgiveness and atonement," I told him, wondering how to get a quorum together as smoothly as possible.

I couldn't believe he would do it, but the next thing I knew, Jerry was calling his friends to come down to the cemetery. He began working the phones as only Jerry knew how to. I anxiously watched as Jerry grabbed a piece of paper from his pocket and start frantically writing and rewriting, all while tears were gushing from his eyes.

In no time at all, his friends started arriving from all over the city. Fancy Mercedes and Jaguars began pulling up in the parking lot of the cemetery. It was moving to see Jerry's upper crust associates arrive to give a helping hand to their good friend.

Surrounded by the growing crowd, Jerry stood at the side of his father's grave. He wiped his red eyes and began speaking to them from his heart.

"My dear friends," he cleared his voice and began. "I am sure you are all wondering why I invited you to the cemetery of all places, and on such short notice. To make a long story short, my dear rabbi, who is standing here beside me, just informed me that it is never too late to ask for forgiveness from a loved one, even posthumously, if it is done at their grave and in the presence of a quorum of ten men."

There was a rustle in the crowd. All eyes were on Jerry as he continued his speech.

"Thus, I have asked all of you, my good friends, to join me in this unusual ritual, to help me receive needed forgiveness from my father. I thank each one of you for coming. Many of you surely know that my father died before I had a chance to iron out a number of distressing issues that continue to haunt me. So here we go." Jerry made his announcement and then paused, rummaging in his pocket.

After a few moments, Jerry pulled out the crumpled piece of paper that he had just written, along with his father's faded picture. He faced the grave, addressing his father directly, glancing at his notes.

"Dear Dad, wherever you are,

"As you can see, I have invited my closest friends, many whom you knew personally. Your friend, the rabbi here, told me that it is written in our holy tradition that inviting them to your grave can help us work things out. So, I really hope you are listening to me, Dad.

"I know that, at times, I have been an impetuous son. Even after experiencing the horrors of the Holocaust, you, Father, tried so hard to give me everything a son could only dream of. You gave me a superior education, you provided me a source of livelihood, and you gave me a beautiful home to grow up in. I, on the other hand, was an ungrateful son, who never reciprocated your magnanimous parenting. "Furthermore, I disappointed you by never following in the footsteps that you dreamed I would follow. Sadly, all I gave you in return was aggravation and heartache," Jerry said, holding back sobs as his body shook with grief. He took a deep breath in, before continuing with his apology.

"And then, a combination of my selfishness, narcissism, and addiction to success caused me to let you down dismally, when I failed you with my life and money choices. How could I have been so insensitive? I am so sorry, Dad, for not respecting your feelings, and for hurting you so profoundly," Jerry said with deep emotion, his body heaving with every word. Close friends moved near him, reaching out to comfort his shaking body.

Jerry wiped his eyes and then said, "All I can say is that I was young, immature, and stupid at the time, and I acted impulsively. Please give me another chance, Father. Please forgive me…please!" Jerry broke down. He began sobbing uncontrollably, with tears rolling down his cheeks. His friends dabbed their eyes with monogrammed handkerchiefs. I felt Morris's presence hovering, and I wondered if Jerry could feel it, too.

Then Jerry continued his emotional monologue, barely pronouncing the rest of the words:

"Dad, I know that it's too late to change the past. But going forward at least, my dear father, I want to express to you my heartfelt, unconditional remorse and to give you an ironclad promise that I will be a far more sensitive person because of this experience, and I will work diligently on becoming a little more of the man you were hoping I would be."

As I listened to Jerry's heartfelt apology, I noticed a beautiful red robin flying overhead, contrasting with the clear blue skies and casting a shadow over us as we stood at the cemetery. I felt, deep down, that Morris was listening to his son's every word with great satisfaction.

As his friends patted him on the back and then paid respects to Morris, Jerry eventually turned his attention back to me. "*Nu*, Rabbi, did I do this forgiveness thing right?" he asked across the crowd.

I gave him a thumbs up, imagining Morris smiling down at us from on high.

After Jerry's friends had left the cemetery, we walked in silence to the parking lot. His gait seemed lighter than it had been these past months. In contrast to his appearance when I first met him in the morning, Jerry looked very much relieved. I could see that a major load of guilt had been lifted from his chest.

"OK, Rabbi. Enough talk about the grave," said Jerry. "Now I need some positive connectivity. You mentioned before that there are other portals besides the grave through which I could communicate with my father. Can you teach me about other portals to his soul?"

"Sure, Jerry. There are a few."

I motioned to Jerry to join me as I sat down on a comfortable looking bench near the parking lot.

'One powerful way to connect to the soul of our loved ones is through their writings. When we read and meditate over the manuscripts left behind by a loved one, we can connect to them on an extremely profound level. In the surviving manuscripts of a departed person, you can discover their soul because the author of the manuscript infuses a segment of his or her soul in their writings during their lifetime," I told him.

"The soul is present in someone's writings?" Jerry questioned.

"Think about the Bible, which is the most popular manuscript in the history of the world. Year after year it's a best seller —and for good reason. In this book we find not only sheer divine brilliance and timeless ethical messages, but a glimpse of its elusive author, the Infinite Creator of Heaven and earth, who like all authors, infused his soul into his manuscript, so to speak," I explained.

"Sounds interesting," Jerry said. "Not sure I totally follow, though."

"This infusion of the Divine Soul into the Hebrew Bible is alluded to in the very first Hebrew word of the Ten Commandments. The very first line of the Ten Commandments is: "I am your G–d, Who has taken you out of Egypt from the house of bondage." The Hebrew word for "I am" is the unusual word *Anochi*, which is Egyptian in etymological origin—not an originally Hebrew word," I continued.

"That's strange," Jerry noted. "Didn't G–d want us to be free of Egyptian influences? That's what I remember from Hebrew school."

"It's a great question, Jerry. Why this unusual choice of words? Why throw an Egyptian word into the most important section of the Hebrew Bible?" I echoed.

"*Nu*, Rabbi," Jerry said. "What's the reason?"

"The Talmud explains that the Egyptian Anochi was chosen because it also serves as an acrostic for the Hebrew words, "I infuse my soul in my writings."

"Interesting," Jerry said. "There are so many hidden meanings in seemingly simple biblical words."

"Yes, in the very first word of Judaism's "Top Ten" list, G–d—like any other author who would invest himself in his or her book—bares His soul in the pages of the Scriptures for all to see," I added.

"So, G–d infuses His 'book' with His infinite, unfathomable, incomprehensible soul," Jerry reflected.

"Yes, the bottom line is that anyone embarking on a journey in search of G–d need not look for exotic addresses. They can simply find Him in the 'book of books.' If one wishes to discover the transcendental elusive Creator of Heaven and earth, let him just take a peek into His runaway best-seller, the Bible," I said, chuckling.

Jerry laughed too. It was the biggest laugh I'd heard from him since his father died.

"The same applies to our loved ones. They, too, can be found in the pages of their writings because that is where they have invested the very essence of their being," I shared.

"How can you compare a parent's casual writings with the Bible?" asked Jerry.

"For many years, I had the honor of transcribing and print-ing a notebook of writings left behind by my grandfather, a legendary rabbi. The pages of his manuscript were so old and brittle that any excessive movement would instantly turn the pages into crumbs, and these priceless treasures that he left behind could have been lost forever. This was an awesome responsibility, but I loved every minute of it," I shared. "Every time I would open my grandfather's notebook, I would be taken over by a wave of inner satisfaction and contentment. And while the work was intellectually stimulating, the joy was not from discovering his original ideas or thinking style. It was more about discovering an emotional relationship.

"That's interesting," Jerry said, listening closely. "What made you feel that way?"

"I would imagine what my grandfather was experiencing when he was writing these pages, and then literally relive it. In his notebook I would find a coffee stain on the paper, a cigarette burn, or a piece of hair from his beard. I was experiencing a total sensory connection to my past through these aged manuscripts," I described.

"I feel like this needs another story, Rabbi," Jerry said with a smile.

"You know me well, Jerry," I said, as I recounted the follow-ing tale:

> On his deathbed, Rabbi Sholom Dovber, the fifth Rebbe of the Chabad rabbinic dynasty, called his son, Rabbi Yosef Yitzchak, the soon-to-be sixth Rebbe, and told him, "I'm going now to Heaven, but I am leaving my writings for you."

"I wonder what he meant by that," Jerry mused.

"The intent of the dying Rebbe was to inform not just his son, who later became his successor, but all of his followers and future followers that by studying his writings, they could maintain a personal connection with him even as he is remotely residing in Heaven," I explained.

"If I only would have known this earlier!" Jerry exclaimed. "In his later years, my mother recently told me, my father had started to write memoirs from his youth, especially of the Holocaust years, but he never quite managed to finish them.

Now I have these stacks of unfinished writings left over from my dad. Maybe I should publish them in his memory and make the connection?"

"Wow, Jerry: that's a great idea! I bet you'll discover a new and meaningful channel to your father." I was elated that Jerry was so open to the idea of publishing his father's memoirs. I wanted to help in any way I could.

"OK, so writing will be a great way to connect to my dad," Jerry summed up. "Are there any other ways?" Jerry seemed very keen to find more ways to expand his connectivity!

"There are many portals. In fact, another portal is in the house of the deceased," I said.

"I thought that when the soul transitions to Heaven, it leaves the house behind," Jerry noted.

"Just as the grave and the remnants of the body serve as a portal to the soul, so does the house where the person lived and studied during the course of their lifetime. Because our loved ones invested during their lifetime quality soul time in a particular residence, their aura still remains there. Through spending quality time in that place of residence or study, we can make powerful connections to the soul that remains intimately connected to that space beyond its physical lifetime," I told him.

"Have you experienced anything like this, Rabbi?" Jerry asked, a look of intense curiosity on his face.

"I remember the Lubavitcher Rebbe, my mentor, always speaking about 770 Eastern Parkway—the famous home and synagogue of the previous Rebbe, his saintly father-in-law. The

Rebbe would insist that you could feel the deceased Rebbe's presence in the building. The Rebbe would spend the rest of his life teaching in that building, never leaving it because of that connection. He always spoke about the incredible power present in that building, and that his father-in-law's presence was palpably felt there," I shared.

"I have felt my father's presence in his house," Jerry commented.

I wondered what Morris's widow — Anna, Jerry's mother, who was living in the house — would think of the portal idea. Did she feel an innate connection to her late husband by virtue of living in the house? And would this mystical idea impact her decision about selling their home?

"Jerry, the same applies, believe it or not, to the physical belongings and clothing of the deceased," I told him.

"Clothing?" asked Jerry with a mystified look on his face. "You must be kidding me?"

"Yes, Jerry, clothing. Well, you know how people spend a few weeks, or even months, after losing a parent organizing their parent's "affairs"? They go about selling their parents' condominium, their possessions, clothing, and anything else they can liquidate and turn into hard cash. But the truth is that they really should not be selling everything. The dwelling, clothing, and possessions of a deceased person are very much imbued with their soul," I told Jerry, carefully.

"That sounds strange," Jerry commented. "And inconvenient. Shouldn't someone else get the benefit of using the items that are still in good condition?"

"The mystics were careful, even during their lifetime, to guard their garments and possessions so they did not fall into the wrong hands, believing that this could harm their soul," I countered. "Material objects have a spiritual component. I have a story to show what I mean."

"Go for it, Rabbi," Jerry said, urging me on.

Napoleon's advancing armies forced Rabbi Schneur Zalman, known as the Alter Rebbe, to flee his hometown of Liadi. The Rebbe left with sixty wagons carrying his extended family and many of his *Chassidim*, escorted by a troop of soldiers attached to the convoy by express order of the czar.

A few miles out of Liadi, the Rebbe suddenly requested the officers accompanying the convoy to provide him with a light carriage, two good horses, and two armed drivers. Taking along some of his own people, the Rebbe rushed back to Liadi.

Upon arriving at his house, he instructed that a careful search be made to see if any of his personal items had been left behind. After a thorough search, a pair of worn-out slippers, a rolling pin and a kneading bowl were found in the attic. The Rebbe instructed that these items be taken along, and that the house be set on fire. Then he blessed the inhabitants of the town, and quickly departed.

"If material items can have such power during one's life, how much more so after one's death," I exclaimed.

"Is it true that you are not allowed to give away the shoes of the deceased? Sounds like superstition to me," Jerry asked skeptically.

"The shoes of the deceased are especially connected with the soul. People who have visited Auschwitz and other camps are most touched by the piles of shoes on display. Whether it's a child's small shoes, or dirty working shoes, each shoe tells a unique story. More than any other garment, shoes take on the personality of their wearer. The mystics say that one should never give away the shoes of the deceased to a stranger," I continued, elaborating on this esoteric concept.

"Funny, my father had an absolute hang-up with shoes. He would never throw them away. He collected them for years. Maybe it has something to do with the Holocaust, who knows, but he had almost as many shoes as Imelda Marcos," Jerry said in wonder. "I always thought it was an unusual habit."

"Interesting," I said, reaching out to comfort Jerry. His face had paled as he remembered his father again, and we were both transported back to where we were—the cemetery parking lot. I looked at my watch and noticed it was getting late.

"Well, I should let you go, Rabbi," Jerry said, looking at his own watch. "It's just hard to leave here. It feels like I'm leaving my father all over again. And I feel like there is so much more to understand about all of this. You've helped me, Rabbi. You have taught me so much. But I need more. How can I connect once I leave here today?"

"OK, Jerry, just like we discussed the existence of portals in space, there also are portals in time. There are windows of time that give us opportunities to connect to our loved ones in Heaven," I told him, hoping he could feel my compassion and support.

"The *shivah* felt like that," Jerry said, looking down.

"Right, and the next auspicious time will be the *yahrtzeit* (lit., year-time)—the date of the anniversary of the passing of the soul from this physical world. In Kabbalah we are taught that every year, on the anniversary date, the soul transitions to a higher level in the heavens above. Consequently, it showers blessings upon those left behind in this world," I told Jerry. I made a mental note to remind my wife to be in touch with Jerry's family about the *yahrtzeit* preparations.

"Remind me what we do for the *yahrtzeit*, Rabbi," Jerry said, jotting down notes in his phone.

"According to Jewish law, the *yahrtzeit* is commemorated with self-introspection, prayers, fasting, and lighting special *yahrtzeit* candles. We also visit the cemetery. By observing these rituals on the anniversary of a loved one's passing, we access their soul and receive the blessings and energy unleashed by the soul on that auspicious day," I explained.

"My father used to have all sorts of customs around *yahrtzeits*," Jerry added. "I wish I remembered what they were. But there were a lot of candles."

"It reminds me of another rabbi joke," I said. Jerry smiled, and nodded for me to continue.

> Naomi and Ruth are arguing about who has the most religious Jewish family.
>
> "My grandmother was so Orthodox," says Naomi, "that she only drank her tea from a yahrtzeit glass."
>
> "That's nothing," replies Ruth. "My grandmother only drank her tea from a yahrtzeit glass with the candle still in it!"

Jerry chuckled in recognition.

"That's funny, Rabbi," Jerry said. "I feel connected to my Jewish roots when you tell these stories. But there must be yet more ways to connect."

"Well, there is what I call the 'lifecycle' portal," I explained. "These are powerful moments in our lives when we can access dearly departed souls when we mark a milestone in our lives. At those special times, we have newfound potential to break open new vistas to reach our loved ones in Heaven. At special moments in our lives, the power of love and family breaks all barriers between us and our loved ones, even in their posthumous state," I explained.

"That sounds like science fiction," Jerry said. "How does it work?"

"Jewish legend has it that our departed loved ones participate in the weddings of their children and grandchildren. It's a well-known belief that the deceased parents, grandparents and great-grandparents of the bride and groom prepare themselves and come down from their heavenly abode to join in at the wedding celebration of their children and descendants."

"How do they know where and when the party is?" Jerry joked.

"There is an ancient tradition to invite deceased relatives to the wedding by going to the cemetery and leaving a physical invitation at the grave," I told him.

"But Rabbi, isn't that a little cultish, inviting the dead? It sounds to me like summoning the dead!" Jerry said, in disbelief. "Even I know that Jews are not allowed to summon the dead."

"I know what you mean, but obviously we are doing something different from that. Our parents come because they love us, and because they are naturally connected to our souls. The fact is that many say their presence at every wedding is very much felt by all," I said, thinking of how else to clarify these customs.

"I do not recall feeling the presence of dead relatives at my wedding," Jerry said. "I wish I could ask my dad if he did."

"I have spoken with many couples and their parents who claim to have felt the presence of their ancestors at the wedding. They told me that it was as if their deceased relatives were standing with them under the wedding canopy," I said.

"I'm still not sure about *that* portal, Rabbi," Jerry said, patting me on the back. "It sounds too spiritual for me. But, since I'm married, I don't have to worry about it for now. Talking about time, I seem to remember something about the holidays. Is there anything special to do on holidays?"

"Yes, of course, Jerry. It is the Jewish belief that the souls of loved ones return to earth and make contact with their relatives on special holidays. As you surely know, there is a very meaningful memorial prayer, Yizkor, which is recited on the main Jewish holidays by those who have lost a loved one."

"Yes, I've heard of Yizkor," Jerry said confidently. "My father was extremely careful to attend synagogue on holidays so he could recite Yizkor for his family members who were killed in the Holocaust."

"This prayer was instituted to remember the dead and recall their memory, letting our loved ones know that they are never, ever forgotten. On special Jewish holidays, the gates of Heaven are opened, allowing the living to make direct contact with the dead," I told Jerry. I hoped he would be willing to say Yizkor for his father when the next holiday came around.

"What an interesting idea," Jerry mused. "I wonder what it's like in Heaven, as the souls await the service in their honor."

"The Kabbalah teaches that there is a great uproar in the heavens at that time, because all the old souls are dressing up and going to visit their children down on earth for the special holiday prayer," I said, picturing a cartoon version of this spiritual event in my mind's eye.

"Rabbi, this is all very interesting and inspiring, but what if I want to connect without going to the synagogue or the cemetery, or waiting for a special occasion or holiday? Is there still a way to connect here and now, without delay?" Jerry asked plaintively.

"Of course, Jerry. You can connect anywhere in the world through what I would call the 'omnipresent' portal," I told him.

"What's that?"

"There is a profound portal to our loved ones within us. This portal is available to us 24/7," I explained. "Conventional religious or spiritual wisdom tends to think that the natural way to reach out to Heaven is through external connections, through external portals. But the truth is that the most powerful connection that one can make is from our inner portal."

"An inner portal sounds even stranger than deceased relatives hovering over a wedding canopy," Jerry said, bemused. "What on earth do you mean?"

"Growing up, there was one ride in Disney World's Magic Kingdom called, "Adventures through Inner Space." Unlike the usual space fantasy rides, where you traveled into the vastness of outer space, this ride traveled through what they called inner space. In this imaginary world, they would shrink you down to the molecular level, and then to atomic level, and then to the point that you felt smaller than an atom. Then they would show you these massive electrons and neutrons the size of planets, surrounding you in their full glory," I said, praying that my example would be meaningful to Jerry.

Jerry smiled. "Hey, now I wish my parents would have taken me to Disney World when I was a kid."

I continued, "The point of this ride was to give you an understanding and perspective that there is a vast world in inner space, at least as compelling as outer space, if not more."

Jerry motioned for me to continue.

"Likewise, in our spiritual journeys, we tend to be blown away by the vast spiritual cosmos outside of us, but the most potent portals to Heaven are found deep within ourselves," I expounded.

"I need one of your stories to better understand this one, Rabbi," Jerry pushed.

Chaim Nachman Bialik (1873–1934) was a Russian Jewish poet who wrote in Hebrew. Bialik was one of the pioneers of modern Hebrew poetry and came to be recognized as Israel's national poet.

He captures this feeling in his poem, Shirati (My Poetry), where he tries to trace the origin of the sigh, the sob, the krechtz, so frequently found in his poetry. He describes the misery of his childhood: His father died when he was very young, leaving seven young orphans. His mother slaved in a little store, supporting his brothers and sisters. Only in the evening could she begin her cooking, cleaning, and sewing.

Late one night the little boy rose from his bed and saw his mother cooking in the kitchen. In utter exhaustion, she was weeping as she kneaded dough for bread. As she baked by candlelight, her lips moved in prayer, "May I bring up my children to be G–d-fearing. May they be true to the Torah. May they never disgrace me." As she prayed, the tears rolled down her sweet, tired, lonely cheeks. She did not realize it, but her tears mixed with the dough.

Little Chaim Nachman saw this heartrending sight and returned to bed. The next morning he ate this very bread. "As I ate, I swallowed my mother's tears. Part of my mother was in that bread. And now you know why there are tears in my eyes; why there is a sigh in my breast."

"This is the truth of life, Jerry," I continued. "A portion of our parents is implanted within us. Unbeknownst to them, they made indelible impressions on us that have been permanently recorded into our very beings. We eat their tears, and their laughs. We drink their smile or their anger. We consume their joys and frustrations. Their obituaries do not lie buried in some old newspaper. They are recorded, and alive in our hearts and souls.

"In describing death, the Bible frequently uses the phrase, 'He expired, and was gathered into his people.' It says this about Abraham, Isaac, and Jacob, and about many others—David, Solomon, etc.

"What is the meaning of this strange expression, 'He was gathered into his people'?

"There's a subtle message here: when we die, we don't disappear; rather, we are "gathered into the people." That's where we wind up: *in people*. People wind up in people, not in the ground.

"We have a piece of our parents—their very soul—within us. The best place to find them may be within our own psyche, within our own soul.

"The same powerful portal we can access at the cemetery can also be found 'gathered' within us," I said.

Jerry wiped his eyes and reached out for a hug. I held him until he pulled away. We got into our cars and drove away. The whole ride home, all I could picture was Morris and Jerry. Memories of their connection and subsequent conflict consumed my thoughts. I hoped today would be the beginning of peace between them.

Transition and Elevation:
How Can We Help the Soul After Death?

A few months later, Jerry showed up at my office unannounced. He had been visiting me after the weekly morning service every so often. Even after our prior conversations, Jerry expressed that he still carried guilt and anger about his relationship with his father. To cope with these dark feelings, he was considering a visit to Auschwitz, the infamous death camp in Poland that his father, Morris, had survived.

I thought the visit was a good idea. If Jerry saw the devastation of the Holocaust and learned firsthand about the traumatic experiences of his father in his younger years, it would help him understand Morris a bit better.

Jerry knocked on my office door hesitantly. I was surprised because our rapport had been comfortable lately.

"Hi, Rabbi, you have a minute?" Jerry asked.

"Sure, come on in," I answered, inviting him to take a seat.

"I've been giving the trip to Europe a lot of thought. I'd like to travel to Auschwitz, but on one condition." Jerry paused, shifted in his seat, and then continued. "Rabbi, I'd like you to come along. I need your support on this journey."

I had encouraged Jerry to take the trip, and so I acquiesced to accompanying Jerry on this emotional (and hopefully healing) trip.

So the next thing I knew, I was traveling with Jerry and his mother, Anna, to the notorious death camp and crematorium in the Polish town of Oswiecim, known simply by its stark German name: Auschwitz. Jerry's wife stayed behind to help their daughter with the twins and to give Jerry an opportunity to heal from the family's painful past. To that end, Jerry's mother decided to join Jerry on the trip. For Anna, it would be an especially meaningful trip: her first time back to Poland since surviving the war.

Jerry had booked one of the most famous tour guides, an Israeli who was a survivor of the Holocaust himself, to take us around. Jerry booked the finest hotels and carefully arranged every detail, including gourmet kosher food for the duration of our visit. Yet, despite the luxurious accommodations, a sense of sorrow hung in the air. On the first morning at the hotel in Krakow, I found Jerry sitting in a corner of the lobby together with his mother, both looking downcast. Already, being in Poland had opened up so many old wounds, magnifying their loss of Morris. I sat down nearby, preparing myself for the intense day of touring.

Jerry noticed me from the corner of his eye. He waved me closer, and said, "*Nu*, Rabbi, nice to see you here bright and early in Krakow."

"Good morning, Jerry," I said, and nodded hello to Anna.

"We were discussing my father, Rabbi," Jerry said.

I nodded for him to continue.

"I'd like your rabbinic thoughts on whether you think my dad is in a better place and not suffering anymore. I mean, I know that he's done with the tremendous physical suffering he experienced during his lifetime, beginning with the war and the concentration camps and ending with his pain-filled final illness, unfortunately. But how about his spiritual "transition" to the next world? Do you think that may be aggravating him now? If he truly lives on in an afterlife and still has some degree of consciousness, how can I possibly know if Dad is now further traumatized over his being taken away from his family and transitioning into Heaven?"

"Jerry, you are perceptive. It's exactly like you say it is. No soul finds peace immediately. It's a gradual process," I told Jerry and Anna.

"I've never heard of this concept, Rabbi," Anna interjected. "Can you explain the process?"

"When the body is laid to rest at the funeral, its soul counterpart is extricated, and then the soul is catapulted on an arduous journey to Heaven. It must go through a very gradual transformation and acclimatization to its new life up there," I told her.

"I never thought about what death is like for the soul," she said, interested to learn more. She leaned in for me to continue. Jerry rested his arm on his mother's back.

"Imagine yesterday's flight to Krakow or, really, any flight to any destination. First, you need to pack up your bags at home, and take a taxi to the airport. Then, you get out and walk into the terminal to get in line for customs and passport control. After that exhausting and humiliating experience, you need to wait for your plane, stand in a long line to board the plane, find your seat, and take the flight to your desired destination. Once there, you must wait to get off the plane, go through customs and passport control yet again, track down your luggage, hail a taxi and sit in traffic until you finally arrive at your hotel," I said, feeling the stress of the long journey from Canada to Poland. "Basically, by the time you finish this process, you are so exhausted that you truly deserve a vacation from the vacation."

Jerry and Anna both laughed in recognition. It had been a long trip for all of us.

"Arrival in Heaven is pretty much the same. In fact, the reason for the extended mourning period in Jewish tradition is not so much for bereavement purposes, as is widely believed. According to the Jewish mystics, it is a time for commiserating with the travel pains of the departed soul. Mourning is primarily meant to be a time to empathize with the soul's discomfort as it transitions to its new reality in Heaven," I explained.

"Why is it painful, Rabbi?" Anna asked. "Don't we believe the soul is going to a better place?"

"Well, initially, in the first days after death, the soul experiences discomfort associated with being extricated from the physical body, and then from transitioning into the unknown world of the spiritual. After the first few days, the soul is subjected to a cleansing and judgment period—which we spoke about before, Jerry, if you recall—which may last for as long as a full year. Only then can the soul find a degree of peace in Heaven," I told them.

"So Rabbi, if I understand you correctly, my father is going through a challenging period of transition now, and he may even be in spiritual limbo and discomfort?" Jerry said, sounding upset. I saw his gaze move to his mother, to gauge her reaction.

"Rabbi, that is a very disconcerting thought," Anna added. "Morris suffered so much in this life. I don't want him to suffer in the World to Come."

"Is there is anything at all that you can suggest for us to do to help his soul during this difficult transitional period? Is there anything we can do down here on earth to help ease his lonely and arduous journey to Heaven?" Jerry asked. His eyes were searching the room, as if looking for Morris among the tourists and businessmen in the hotel lobby.

"We have been speaking over the last few days about doing something considerable, something for the rabbi personally and for his family in honor of Morris," Anna said in a serious tone. "We are prepared to help his soul in any way possible."

Anna paused, glanced at Jerry and then continued speaking.

"Rest assured, Rabbi," she winked with her wise eyes, "Money is not an issue here. As you know, Morris left us a generous estate, and we are prepared to do whatever it takes to give his soul the peace he deserves."

I appreciated Anna's desire to help her Morris adjust to the afterlife at any cost. And it was beautiful to see Jerry connecting with his mother, in Morris's memory. I felt the trip was a sign of healing for them. But I'd hoped they would be open to spiritual paths of helping Morris's soul, more than a discussion of money.

"It's true, there are plenty of things you can do to help Morris, but, contrary to conventional wisdom, they are primarily spiritual things—not financial. We can't purchase our loved one's place in Heaven. G–d does not accept bribes," I said with a sigh and a soft smile. Their offer was so kind, and yet I knew I had to help them do what was best for Morris's soul. "We can't pay our way into Heaven, and as much as we would like to, we can't take along with us any of our physical possessions after death."

Anna and Jerry both looked surprised at my reaction. They glanced at each other, wondering what to say in response to my refusal. I worried that I had insulted them, but decided to explain with an example from the Bible.

"King David, poet of the Jewish people, put it so eloquently in his book of Psalms:

> "Be not thou afraid when one waxeth rich, when the wealth of his house is increased; for when he dieth he shall carry nothing away: his wealth shall not descend after him. Though while he lived he blessed his soul: 'Men will praise thee, when thou shalt do well to thyself'; it shall go to the generation of his fathers; they shall never see the light. Man that is interested in honor understandeth not; he is like the beasts that perish."

"Basically, King David is saying that all the money in the world won't follow us to Heaven."

"I know my father wasn't able to take his money or possessions with him, but I'm surprised that our monetary support of our dear rabbi here won't make a difference," Jerry said, looking annoyed at my reaction to his offer.

I have a story you may not have heard, Jerry," I replied, "about the aftermath of the death of a twentieth-century Jewish magnate."

This successful man died in Israel after a long illness at the age of 80. He was a real estate tycoon who had become a billion-aire. When he passed away, he left a vast fortune worth billions of dollars. He left two wills, directing that one be opened immediately and that the other one be opened thirty days later. Among the instructions left in his first will was the request that he be buried with a certain pair of socks he owned.

His children immediately brought the socks to the *Chevrah Kadisha*, requesting that their father be buried in them. Of course the *Chevrah Kadisha* refused, reminding the family that it is against Jewish law. They pleaded, explaining that their father was a very pious and learned man, and he obviously had a very good reason to make this request. The *Chevrah Kadisha* remained firm in their refusal.

The family frantically summoned the *Chevrah Kadisha* to the rabbinical court where the great Rav explained to them, "Although your father left that request when he was in this world, now that he is in the world of truth, he surely understands that it is in his best interest to be buried without the socks."

The man was buried without his socks. Thirty days later, the second will was opened and it read something like this: "My dear children, by now you must have buried me without my socks. I wanted you to truly understand that a man can have one billion dollars, but in the end, he can't even take along one pair of socks!"

"Well, they say money can't buy love, and it seems it can't even buy a pass into Heaven," Jerry commented. "Rabbi, you said there are meaningful things that can help my dad's soul. What are these things?"

"When we arrive in Heaven, it's the good deeds that we performed during our lifetime that pave the way. They escort us right into Heaven. The Talmud says, "Whoever performs a good deed in this world, it precedes him for the World to Come; and (on the flip side) whoever commits a transgression in this world, it clings to him and precedes him for the Day of Judgment," I told them.

"Morris did so many good deeds," Anna said.

"He sure did, and whatever good deeds we manage to collect in the course of our lifetime stand us in good stead in Heaven. But once we have completed our so-called "gig" on earth, we cannot continue to gather any more good deeds, and the books of our lives are basically closed," I added.

"There's a story coming, Rabbi," Jerry said warmly. "I can feel it."

"OK," I conceded. "Here's a story to illustrate the point."

A very wealthy man not known for his piety stood in a long line of those waiting to have their lives assessed by the Heavenly court. He listened attentively as those who were being judged before him recounted both their spiritual failings and their achievements. A number of them seemed to have the scales weighed against them, until they suddenly remembered acts of charity they had performed, which dramatically tipped the scales in their favor. The rich man took it all in and smiled to himself.

When it was his turn, he confidently said, "I may have committed many sins during my lifetime, but I realize now what has the power to override them. I am a very wealthy man and I will be happy to write out a very large check to whichever charity you recommend."

To which the court replied, "We are truly sorry, but here in Heaven we do not accept checks — only receipts."

Anna and Jerry chuckled. "Morris gave so much charity," Anna said proudly.

"Yes, he has a lot of receipts to turn in up there" I said, connecting Morris and the story. All of a sudden, I missed Morris terribly.

"So, tell me more about how this Heavenly bank account works, Rabbi," Anna said. "I want to understand."

"When we are born, a new account opens in the Heavenly bank, and gives us a deposit book and a checkbook. The deposit book is to record the good deeds we perform throughout our lifetime, and the checkbook is for withdrawals, paid out in good health and prosperity," I explained. "When we die, our account is closed, and all we can do in Heaven is use the deposits we have saved over the years. The good deeds, amassed in the course of our lifetime, can be withdrawn and enjoyed in the World to Come. But there are no more deposits," I told them.

Jerry and Anna nodded. And then Jerry spoke up. "You said there were ways we could help my father's soul transition smoothly into its Heavenly existence."

"Yes, there is one exception to this 'no deposit' rule," I shared.

"What's that, Rabbi?" Jerry asked quietly.

"The good deeds that continue to be performed by our children!" I exclaimed. "Even though we can't physically continue doing good deeds ourselves after we die, and our personal depositing is over, our children's deeds are attributed to us because of our influence on them during our lifetime," I said, hoping the point was clear. "Through the good deeds of our children, we continue to inspire and change the world, even after we die. This is our spiritual legacy that continues to fill our account in Heaven, and we reap the dividends of those good deeds indefinitely."

"See how lucky we are to have you Jerry, our *Kaddishel*," Anna said, leaning warmly toward her only son.

"But what about someone who has no children, Rabbi?" Jerry questioned.

"Good question, Jerry. It's not only our children, but in fact anyone we have positively influenced. Whether it's a friend, a neighbor, or a student, we continue to receive credit for the good deeds of our protégés forever and ever," I clarified.

149

"OK, Rabbi, so what's the bottom line?" Jerry pressed. "What can I do to help my father's soul?"

"We can help our parents by continuing to live our lives in a way that reflects well on them. Good deeds help mitigate the severity of their judgment on high, and on their journey to Heaven. In other words, when our parents die, we don't only ask what our parents have bequeathed to us, we also need to ask what we can bequeath to our parents." I explained.

"But are you trying to make us feel guilty here? Are you implying that if my father doesn't have quite the Heaven he expected it is *my* fault? Isn't the belief that every person is responsible for himself?" Jerry sounded distressed and angry. "I flew here, didn't I? I'm facing my father's history to heal."

"Yes, you're doing a lot for him. All I am saying is that while your father is primarily judged on his own merits, there is room for extra credits that can come from you, his only son. You are considered one of your father's crowning achievements of his lifetime," I told him.

"Now I hear you, Rabbi," said Jerry. "That is food for thought."

I was about to jump in with ideas when Jerry began to speak again.

"Rabbi, we know how your synagogue is struggling financially, and we would love to share with you, and help you," Jerry said with a warm smile. "It's a cause my father loved. Would that be a worthy good deed?"

"Of course, that's very generous and kind of you to think of the synagogue. It's not the same without Morris handing out candy to the kids," I said, moved that they wanted to contribute to the synagogue Morris had attended for thirty years. And certainly, a donation would help with the renovations. If they only knew how much I could use that help!

"Showing up with lollipops kept him going," Anna said. "We'd love to contribute."

I was just about to respond, when in walked the famous Israeli tour guide, a fellow by the name of Avraham Eisen.

"Are you the Goldshtein group from Ottawa?" Avraham asked us with a very thick Polish Jewish accent.

Anna and Jerry nodded yes.

"I used to have a good friend when I was in Auschwitz with that very same name. Do you perhaps know my good old friend Moishe Goldshtein who lives in Ottawa?"

Jerry's eyes popped. "You knew Moishe Goldstein? He was my father, Morris, of blessed memory. Remarkable!"

"Yes, he was a good friend of mine from the olden days. We lived through this Auschwitz ordeal together, you know. We bonded there," Avraham explained. "And did I hear you say that your father passed away? So sorry to hear that. Oy, he was a good man, your father, but let me tell you that he lived through hell on earth."

"Wow," said Jerry. "I can't believe that I am taking a tour of Auschwitz with my father's good friend. Avraham, I need you to tell me everything you know about my father, and what he lived through."

"Everything?" he chuckled. "I am not sure you want to hear everything about Auschwitz. They used to say that what happens in Auschwitz stays in Auschwitz, but I will try my best, obviously."

We all got into the car and made our way to Auschwitz from Krakow. It was estimated to be an hour's drive. I took out my book of Psalms to say my daily portion. Avraham began speaking, preparing us for what we were about to see.

"What you are about to experience today has been a life-altering experience for many people. About fifty years ago,

Auschwitz was the epicenter of the greatest evil ever to be perpetrated by humankind in history. Six million Jews were exterminated in a very short period of time as part of a nefarious plan to wipe out the entire Jewish population of Europe, if not the world."

The rest of the hour passed quickly as Avraham pointed out various sights in the Polish countryside. Soon, we arrived at the entrance to Auschwitz-Birkenau. We saw those infamous train tracks that brought hundreds of thousands of Jews in cattle cars, and we shuddered.

Auschwitz! Just the thought of it gave me goosebumps. I had vivid memories of speaking to Morris many times about his horrific experiences there. Sometimes, after reciting Yizkor, he would describe that bleak moment of his arrival to the gates of Auschwitz.

"All I can think about is the story Morris shared every year at the anniversary of his arrival in this place. Everyone in the *shul* was moved to tears when he told it," I said, holding back my own tears.

"Please, tell the story," Anna said quietly. "It will help me to hear it again, here in this horrific place."

"I'll try my best to get the details right," I said to Anna. "Here's how I remember Morris telling the story."

Morris arrived here at Auschwitz with his parents and sisters after a three-day journey in a suffocating cattle cart, filled with the stench of urine and feces of hundreds of people. He couldn't wait to get out. Immediately, he jumped off the train and was directed by the soldiers and the blaring loudspeakers to step into a line in front of high-ranking officers of the German Nazi establishment. This was his first encounter with the infamous "angel of death," Doctor Mengele himself.

Mengele looked at him with his piercing cold eyes, inspected him from head to toe, and told him casually, "You look like a very strong, capable young man." Mengele casually pointed his crooked finger to the left, sending Morris to a labor camp, which meant that he had a chance to live. Morris's parents and siblings were not as fortunate. They were in the same line, but unlike Morris, they were sent by Mengele in the opposite direction, which—unbeknownst to them—was to the notorious gas chambers and crematoria.

Morris barely caught a glimpse of his family on that fateful day as they were taken away to their cruel deaths. He lamented many times over how guilty he felt when he found out about their different fate. As a young teen, all he was thinking about was survival, and not his family. He felt guilty that he failed to take one last look in their direction."

"I can't even start to imagine what that must have felt like," Jerry said, his voice choked up.

"Your father never forgot that lapse for the rest of his life," Anna said sadly. "He told me how he regretted his lack of focus at that moment. He didn't realize it would later become an important link to retracing his past and his perished family," I added.

"Wow, Rabbi," said Jerry sadly. "I truly regret that I didn't listen to my father's stories in his lifetime. My father used to repeat his stories many times, but when I was young I was busy with my friends and my career. Stories from the old man were the last thing on my mind. *Oy*, Rabbi, if only I had paid more attention!" Jerry shared.

"You and your father are more alike than you will ever know," I said. "Both of you share that guilty feeling over not paying more attention in the past."

Anna nodded in affirmation of my assessment. Over the past months of getting to know Jerry, I had noticed how similar he was to Morris.

Avraham, the tour guide, led us into the camp, passing under the notorious gates of Auschwitz. The ominous sign above the entrance said, *Arbeit Macht Frei*, which means, "Work will set you free." It was under those gates that so many people's fate was determined, Avraham told us.

"Those who were lucky enough to pass those gates and survive the selection process were given a sentence of back-breaking labor in the concentration camp. This gave them a small chance to come out alive," he explained. All of us nodded along. So far, it was a familiar, painful history.

"Morris made it beyond this point, as he survived the war. But, let me tell you, it wasn't easy," Avraham said, turning to Anna. "You know from personal experience."

Anna shook her head in recognition. A strong woman, Anna rarely showed emotions openly, but she dabbed at her eyes.

"You had to be extremely resourceful to survive. Every day that we survived was a miracle," she added.

"We had to do the most ridiculous things, me and your father, just to live," Avraham added. "You see that barracks over there?" Avraham pointed to this long austere looking red rectangular building, "This is where your father and I slept in our first year in Auschwitz. Come, let me show you."

We walked toward the bunker. Avraham brought us inside and showed us the infamous beds where the inmates slept. "Imagine hundreds of people fitting in here. We were literally packed like sardines."

I looked at the meager bunks in dismay. Jerry had his arm on his mother's shoulders, supporting her through this emotional tour.

"Every morning they would wake us up at 5 a.m. to call us out to the field there," Avraham said, pointing to a large open space nearby. "And take attendance. We would wait sometimes hours until the last inmate was accounted for. Because many people didn't survive through the night, it took quite a while for them to account for every inmate."

Avraham then led us to an eerie looking plot of land beside the notorious gas chambers and crematorium. There were only remnants of the original structures left.

"This is holy ground," he said, standing with a silent reverence.

"What do you mean?" asked Jerry.

"We know that there were close to one million bodies burned in this one place. I remember the smell like today. There was a stench of flesh burning here and ashes galore. The ashes were all over the place. The ashes would fly like snowflakes in the wind and land right where you are standing," Avraham described.

Anna looked like she might faint from the memory of being in this place. Jerry held his mother up gently, and bowed his head in respect.

Avraham continued, "I remember your father distinctly telling me, just after he arrived in Auschwitz, how weird it felt knowing that the ashes of his parents and family who were taken to the crematorium may be right here on this field."

"My whole family right here! An invisible cemetery right under our feet!" Jerry exclaimed. "What meaningful tribute can we make standing in the presence of my dead family?"

Anna swayed with emotion.

"Kaddish, Jerry," asserted Avraham. "Say the Kaddish— the Jewish memorial prayer: you know it. Say it right here, right now. Do it for the memory of your father and the ashes of his family. We have a quorum of ten men if we join with another group, so we can say the Kaddish."

The Kaddish (memorial prayer) is one of the most recognized congregational prayers of the Jewish tradition. It is typically recited by the children of the deceased at the funeral, and then every day for the entire year thereafter, and every year on the anniversary of the death. Jerry had recited it at Morris's funeral, once more at the *shivah*-week breakfast, and a few more times during the following months.

Kaddish is also said on special occasions. Avraham was thinking just like me, that standing here at the biggest Jewish cemetery in the world surely qualified for the recital of the memorial prayer.

"Kaddish?" said Jerry, shaking. His face went white. "Not sure if I feel like saying that quite yet. This is way too emotional for me here and I don't know if I am quite up to it."

I appreciated that Jerry did not feel emotionally ready for this. I really wanted him to say the Kaddish, as I thought it would be both therapeutic and meaningful for him, but I didn't want to push him.

Anna spoke up instead: "Do you remember your father's favorite nickname for you?"

"Yes," said Jerry. "I remember. He called me his *Kaddishel.*"

"Do you know where this strange nickname comes from, Jerry, and why your father called you by that unusual name?" I asked.

"Dad explained to me that in the old country, they used to call an only son a "Kaddishel" because their son would be the one to carry on their legacy by saying the Kaddish memorial prayer," Jerry answered.

"You really recited the Kaddish in Hebrew beautifully at your father's funeral. You said it like a pro," I told Jerry. Anna nodded with pride.

"Thanks," said Jerry. "Truth be told, Rabbi, before the funeral I practiced reading it all night long. It felt gratifying saying it for my old man that day. While I didn't have any idea what the words meant, they somehow touched me very deeply. The words of the prayer had a stirring quality. It felt like some kind of spiritual comforting mantra."

"Jerry, you could say it for us here in Auschwitz," I urged.

"I don't know if I feel up to it. Please don't pressure me into this, Rabbi," Jerry said, sounding stressed.

I felt bad putting the pressure on him. "I hear you, Jerry. It's just something to consider when you feel ready."

"Thank you, Rabbi. Maybe it would help me if I could understand more about the prayer."

I nodded, and motioned for him to continue. Avraham stood, respectfully waiting, and Anna looked interested to find out more about the Kaddish prayer.

"What would you like to know?" I asked, praying I'd have an answer for him.

Jerry responded, reluctantly, "After reading the prayer, I hope this doesn't sound disrespectful, but it really makes no sense why the Kaddish prayer was chosen for mourners when, in my humble opinion, there is nothing in it that offers any real comfort."

I had wondered about that too, when I had been studying to be a rabbi.

Jerry continued: "On the surface, it seems like another typical "Praise the L–rd" prayer that extols G–d's virtues. Frankly, it sounds like a serious Divine ego trip to me."

Jerry's face reddened as he shared his thoughts.

"This prayer bothered me so much that when I came home after the funeral, I went straight to my prayer book. I read and reread the translation of Kaddish many times, hoping to find solace in this vague poetic prayer. And you know what? Nothing. I still don't get it. There isn't the slightest hint to death or mourning in the entire prayer, and certainly nothing about the afterlife. It makes no sense to me why we remember and honor our loved ones with a prayer that ignores them, and just talks about G–d." He paused, out of breath after this emotional outpouring.

"Good question, Jerry. You are right. The famous Jewish mourner's prayer makes no reference to death or the afterlife, and it offers nothing in terms of comforting the mourner as we would expect it to do," I began.

Jerry and Anna looked expectantly, awaiting answers I hoped I could provide. "But what Kaddish does offer is something far greater. It offers an opportunity to reaffirm the mourner's faith in life after experiencing their devastating loss. When we lose a parent or another loved one, we become prone to losing our faith and giving up on life altogether."

"Yes, that is true for me," Anna responded quietly. "It has been difficult to go on."

"Kaddish is a statement to the community that, despite the dark challenges, the mourner stands strong and maintains his faith. It's basically a reaffirmation of faith in our darkest hour," I explained.

"I still don't relate to it," Jerry said sadly.

"I am sure that you are familiar with the unusual Jewish custom of washing one's hands when leaving the cemetery. In many Jewish cemeteries they build a washing basin at the exit."

"Yes, I've always found that a bit strange," Jerry admitted.

"The reason for washing the hands is not because death is dirty or impure, but because of the devastating impact that death has on one's soul and most importantly on one's faith. Death naturally breeds doubt and confusion. Washing hands upon leaving the cemetery symbolically cleanses us from the negativity of death," I told them. Anna shook her head in understanding, while Jerry maintained a skeptical expression.

"That's a little dramatic, no?" Jerry said.

"When a mourner returns from the cemetery, their whole life crumbles in front of their eyes. For many, gnawing doubts challenge their faith to the very core. Why did my loved one pass away? Why now?"

"So how does Kaddish help?" Jerry challenged.

"Kaddish works like a form of bereavement therapy. Instead of instinctively sulking and becoming angry at the world for your loss, Jewish tradition compels you to publicly reaffirm your faith in life, and in G–d. This is so important, especially at the vulnerable moment of experiencing personal loss," I said, hoping to shed light on this important prayer."

"OK, so I said Kaddish at the funeral," Jerry said, looking down at the ground. "Why here?"

"Saying Kaddish here, in Auschwitz, the darkest place in the world, is an act of reaffirming life inside the Nazi headquarters," I said, feeling the energy of the perished souls. This was holy ground.

"The Rabbi is right." said Avraham. "I remember your father saying Kaddish here in Auschwitz for his friends and family many times."

"But Rabbi," insisted Jerry. "I still don't feel good about saying this dark prayer in this dark place. To me, saying the Kaddish is just echoing words that were said out of desperation, when there was little hope. Are we just echoing the song of a battered and decimated generation that couldn't stand up for themselves, so they resorted to esoteric prayers?"

"Your father and his generation of survivors weren't losers. They were the real winners," I clarified, "even if we can't understand how they managed to withstand the horror and loss of the war."

"What do you mean, Rabbi?" Jerry asked. "My father lived —so that means he won, so to speak. But when he was here?"

"For the Jews who witnessed their relatives massacred and shot by Nazi soldiers, who starved and worked and struggled here, it may have seemed at the time like the Nazis were the winners and we were the losers," I said, picturing the starving prisoners facing cruel Nazi guards.

"*Nu*," Jerry said. "Keep going."

"In reality, the Nazis had to live the rest of their lives with their sadistic choices and, on the other hand, we—our people—lived with peace of mind knowing that under the most dire circumstances, we still managed to keep our morality and dignity intact, never yielding to or becoming the demons who oppressed us," I shared.

"Jerry, your father looked the Nazi enemy straight in the eye and projected the aura of a winner, never a loser," Avraham reassured.

"Yes, he and his generation were beaten to a pulp, but they were the winners, hands down," I added.

"No one imagined we would survive," Anna shared. "No one could imagine the strong Nazis losing the war."

"I remember the story your father was fond of telling, about the grand Rabbi of Klausenberg, Romania," I told them.

After the Nazis invaded that small village, they began to celebrate the defeat of the Jews in their usual sadistic fashion. They gathered the Jews into a circle in the center of town, and then paraded their Rebbe, Rabbi Yekusiel Yehudah Halberstam (1905–1994), into the center.

The Klausenberger Rebbe was later taken to Auschwitz, where his wife and 11 children perished. The SS guards began taunting and teasing the Klausenberger Rebbe, pulling his beard and pushing him around. The vile soldiers trained their guns on him as the commander began to speak. "Tell us Rabbi," sneered the officer, "do you really believe that you are the Chosen People?"

The soldiers guarding the crowd howled in laughter. But the Rebbe did not. In a serene voice, he answered loud and clear, "Most certainly."

The officer became enraged. He lifted his rifle above his head and sent it crashing on the head of the Rebbe. The Rebbe fell to the ground. There was rage in the officer's voice. "Do you still think you are the Chosen People?" he yelled.

Once again, the Rebbe nodded his head and said, "Yes, we are." The officer became infuriated. He kicked the Rebbe in the chin and repeated: "You stupid Jew, you lie here on the ground, beaten and humiliated, in a puddle of blood. What makes you think that you are the Chosen People?"

With his mouth gushing blood, the Rebbe replied. "As long as we are not the ones kicking, beating and murdering innocent people, we are the chosen people!"

"The Klausenberg Rebbe survived the war and came to America, where he remarried, had more children, and built a grand Chassidic movement. He also built the beautiful Laniado hospital in Netanya, Israel," I added, moved by this story of courage in the place where the events actually happened.

"What a story, Rabbi," Jerry exclaimed. "What courage."

"This is precisely what Kaddish is all about. It's an affirmation of our faith. It is a prayer filled with hope and optimism. It is a prayer of winners. Your father and his surviving friends were the winners of Auschwitz, Jerry," I said with all the strength and emotion that filled me.

Avraham nodded, and Anna held back tears. Avraham opened the prayer book to the right page, and Jerry began cautiously reciting the Kaddish for the memory of his father. I felt Morris's presence in the air as Jerry read the ancient Hebrew-Aramaic words of the prayer.

"*Yitgadal Veyitkadash...*" Jerry recited the entire prayer.

It was a powerful moment in time. The world stood still in Auschwitz that day. Afterwards, Jerry broke down and began sobbing uncontrollably. His sobbing reverberated across the open fields of Auschwitz-Birkenau.

At that moment, in the callous killing fields of Auschwitz, I could hear, between the words of the prayer, a sense of reconciliation. Jerry was proud of his father and, perhaps for the first time, understood the context of his father's life and why his father may have at times lost it with him, especially in his later years.

It was an emotional moment, and after a moment of quiet reverence, Avraham, the tour guide, continued to explain the significance of the place.

"This place right here is where your father and I spent many months before we were liberated," Avraham shared.

"What were you doing here?" asked Jerry, who sounded more engaged and curious than before.

"Taking care of our brethren. Giving them the honor they deserved by saying Kaddish for them," Avraham told us.

"What kind of honor could you mean in this hell on earth?" Jerry said angrily.

"Well, Jerry, unfortunately there were many people who committed suicide here, rather than living out their wretched lives. Some chose to electrocute themselves on the barbed wire fence surrounding the camp, while others tried to escape and were shot to death by those Nazi bastards. Burying them, that was part of our job," Avraham told us, making the empty barracks feel especially sad.

"So you helped the Nazis?" Jerry challenged.

"Not really, Jerry, we gave honor to the victims," Avraham said calmly.

"But you still helped them," Jerry repeated. Anna gave her son a stern look.

Avraham maintained his composure, and then responded. "No, Jerry. While some prisoners worked in the field and others were digging rocks, we removed the dead bodies. I wouldn't call that working for the Nazis. Or, you could say in a sense that all the prisoners worked for the Nazis."

"I can't believe this," Jerry cried out. "Are you telling me that father, my holy father, was one of the Sonderkommandos? My father, who I thought was so perfect, the man I just said Kaddish for, was a Nazi henchman? I can't believe what I am hearing from you, Avraham. And you, too: shame on you!" Jerry was totally caught by surprise, and so were we all. Anna paled at this revelation.

Sonderkommandos were prisoners, usually Jews, who were forced, on threat of their own deaths, to aid with the disposal of gas chamber victims during the Holocaust.

"No Jerry, never," said Avraham firmly. "We were nothing of the sort. Sonderkommandos maybe, but Nazi henchman, no!"

Jerry shook his head in contempt, while Anna held onto Jerry's arm for support. I wasn't sure what to say in this delicate situation. I knew the war complicated everything.

After a pause, Avraham decided to describe what it was like during the war. "Do you have any idea what it takes to survive when you are starving for months without end? Survival makes you do all kinds of things," Avraham said.

"But, still, I don't know," Jerry said, hands on his hips in judgment.

"Jerry, do you have any idea how many people were actually saved because of people like your father and myself? We made it our business to let the people coming of those wretched train rides to Auschwitz know what they were up against, and how to save themselves from the wicked Dr. Mengele's *selektzia*. Not much of a choice, but those sent to the concentration camps at least had a chance to survive, in contrast to the gas chamber where they faced certain death," Avraham said, in a plaintive voice that pushed us to hear him out, to give the benefit of the doubt.

"Yes, the second job of this 'chosen' group of Sonderkommandos was to confiscate and organize the suitcases of the new arrivals to Auschwitz. While performing their duty, many Sonderkommandos would give a "heads-up" of what was about to befall their fellow Jews. And sometimes they were able to impart lifesaving advice," Avraham continued.

Jerry was listening carefully to Avraham. We all were. Anna relaxed her grip on Jerry's arm for a moment. I wondered what would transpire next.

"If not for us, so many more would have died," Avraham exclaimed.

"I can't believe that my father, before whom I felt so small and unworthy, was a regular prisoner, who buried his fellow Jews, swept their ashes, and worst of all, was probably looked down upon by some of his brethren as a collaborator," Jerry said in disbelief.

'Here I am saying Kaddish in honor of a father who was a traitor of his people. And here, I thought that I was coming to Auschwitz to understand my father, and now I know him even less!" Jerry said with disgust in his voice.

We were all shocked. We all stood there stunned. Jerry was visibly hurting. Avraham was embarrassed. There was a deafening silence, as no one could think of anything to say. What was there to say? Standing right in front of us was a humiliated Holocaust survivor and guide, who was being accused of being a traitor, of committing crimes against his own people, and for exposing the dubious past of my best friend, my mentor and Jerry's father, Morris. It was a devastating moment, and not the experience I had wished for Jerry and Anna. Everyone stood frozen in their place. It was like time itself had stopped.

Finally, I broke the silence.

"No, Jerry, you are wrong," I said as gently as I could. "You need to be forgiving and understanding of your father. Look around at this death camp, and see the answer for yourself. Look at this house of horrors, and see precisely what your father had to survive. He lived a tortured and complex life."

"It's hard to imagine my gentle father in such a horrible role," Jerry said. "And here I am honoring him, when the truth of his life was so complicated."

"We are taught to pray for the dead, and not begrudge them. The mystics say that the recital of Kaddish is not only for the benefit and rehabilitation of the living, but mostly to help alleviate the anguish of the dead. By saying Kaddish, we ease the suffering of the departed soul as it transitions into the next world, and we help it deal with the torment of its life choices. Kaddish elevates the soul of the deceased and helps the soul move on.

"So he sanctimoniously judged my life choices and decisions, yet I should be accepting?" Jerry asked with bitterness.

"It's ironic: here you thought that you need your father's forgiveness, when he really needs yours," I said softly.

"How can I forgive him for his role in the war?" Jerry said. "How can I move past this revelation?"

"If you, his son, won't understand him and forgive him, who will forgive him, Jerry?" I asked him, sincerely hoping he could find a way to help Morris's soul. "He needs you now, more than you will ever know."

"OK, Rabbi, I did it. I said Kaddish for him, pushing past all my boundaries and anger, only to find out my old man was a traitor. I prayed for a man that, it seems, might not have deserved it."

I looked Jerry straight in the eyes. "Stop being so sanctimonious and judgmental of your father, Jerry. The Talmud tells us that the first Kaddish ever recited for the memory of a deceased person came about for a soul that needed serious help."

"Please tell us, Rabbi," Anna interjected. I was not sure if she was really interested in the history of Kaddish or to diffuse the awkward and embarrassing moment. "Yes, Rabbi, I want to hear the history of Kaddish."

Rabbi Akiva, one of the greatest teachers in the days of the Talmud, was walking through a cemetery when he saw a naked man, black as charcoal, carrying a large pile of wood and hurrying like a horse.

"Stop!" the rabbi ordered him. And the man stopped.

"What is with you?" demanded Rabbi Akiva, "What is this harsh labor of yours? If you are a slave and your master is so harsh, then I will free you. And if you are poor, let me make you wealthy."

The man answered, "Please, Rabbi, do not delay me! My supervisors may become very angered if I am late!"

Rabbi Akiva responded, "Who are you, and what do you do?"

The man replied, "I am dead. Every day, they send me to chop wood, upon which they burn me every night."

Rabbi Akiva asked, "And when you were in this world, what was your work?"

"I was a tax collector," the man answered. "I would favor the wealthy and persecute the poor."

"So," asked the rabbi, "have you heard anything from your supervisors about any way you could be redeemed from your punishment?"

"Yes," the man replied. "I heard from them, but it is something that could never happen. They said that if I had a son, and if that son would stand among the congregation and say Kaddish, and the congregation would answer, 'Amen!' Then they could absolve me from my punishment."

"But," he continued, "I did not leave a son behind. True, my wife was pregnant when I died, but I do not know whether she gave birth to a boy. And if she did, who would teach him Torah? I do not have a single friend in the world!"

On the spot, Rabbi Akiva resolved to search for that child. He asked the man for his name.

"My name is Ukba. My wife was Shoshiva. My town was Lanuka'a."

Immediately, Rabbi Akiva set out for that town. When he arrived there, he asked the townspeople about Ukba.

"May his bones grind in Hell!" they replied.

He asked about his wife Shoshiva and they said, "May her name and her memory be erased!"

He asked about her child and they said, "She had a boy, and he is uncircumcised."

The people hated her so much, they hadn't even bothered to circumcise her child.

Without further delay, Rabbi Akiva took this child and circumcised him. He sat the child before him to teach him, but the child would not learn.

So he fasted for forty days. After forty days, a voice came from Heaven: "Rabbi Akiva, why are you fasting?"

He replied, "Master of the Universe! Have I not already made myself a guarantor before You for the lad?"

Immediately, G–d opened the boy's heart and the rabbi was able to teach him how to read Torah and how to say the prayers. Then he stood the boy before the congregation, and he said the prayers, and they answered him. The boy said Kaddish and they answered him, "Amen!"

His father was freed and came straight to Rabbi Akiva in a dream. "Let your heart rest assured that you saved me from the judgment of Hell."

"Kaddish is there to help the soul with its struggles, and it is there especially for a soul that is in need of merits," I told Jerry and Anna, who was listening carefully.

"Jerry, you have the ability to release your father from his past struggles," Anna told her son firmly.

"Interesting story, Rabbi, but do you honestly believe that even I should be forgiving my father? Do you believe it's in my power to truly *help* him? Do you honestly believe that I, the lowly Jerry who spent a lifetime sinning, can honestly help my father with atonement on his spiritual journey?"

"As an only child, you have the unique ability to tip the scales for your father and help him succeed in his travels in the afterlife," I said, encouraging him.

"I just don't know, Rabbi," Jerry hesitated. "What exactly would I need to do to help him at this point?"

"By continuing where your father left off, and accepting the mission statement of the Kaddish, you are a living credit to your father. And despite your colorful past, you can be of a great help to your father in Heaven," I tried explaining.

Avraham the tour guide was standing watching our conversation unfold, He was still visibly shocked by the accusations that Jerry had hurled at him. "It must be a big surprise," Avraham kindly acknowledged. "But Jerry, you should listen to your rabbi. You should know that your father and I tried our best under the circumstances. Your father was the best of men, Jerry. If not for his fight to survive in every possible way, think for a moment: Would you be here today? I agree, Jerry, that it was not a perfect situation. Working for the Nazis could never be a good thing, but what were his options? Listen carefully to what the rabbi said. Pray for your father's soul, and while you are at it, pray for me too! I did what I had to for the sake of my children, too, and I hope that they, too, will have the same compassion and understanding."

Jerry looked like he was about to cry from Avraham's emotional plea. He looked at Anna, who was dabbing the tears in her eyes with a crumpled tissue.

Avraham spoke again, this time in a quiet, pleading tone. "And continue saying Kaddish for your father, Jerry, not only in Auschwitz, but do it more often in the synagogue back home. It is therapeutic for you, and a blessing for your father."

Anna, who was quietly absorbing every word, and surely knew Morris's secret all along, asked, "And what about a wife? Are we not counted? Isn't there anything that I can do to help my husband's tortured soul? I would think," she said, becoming indignant, "that after being married to this husband of mine for over fifty years, I, too, could contribute something to Morris's well-being in Heaven!"

"Of course, Anna," I said, "We all can participate in assisting Morris during his judgment period. Yes, the children, in this case, do contribute the lion's share, but all of us—and especially a spouse, who was her husband's soul mate and inspiration—can positively influence the outcome of his judgment too."

"OK, I can't say Kaddish, though," Anna said.

"Anna, believe it or not, Kaddish is only one small part of what we can do for the soul. I know that in the Jewish community there is a major fuss made about Kaddish recital, as if it is the be-all and end-all. There are many other things we can do for the soul," I explained.

"OK," said Anna. "So, what can *I* do?"

"The mystics write that studying in the merit of deceased is seven times as powerful as the Kaddish. Charity in their honor is extremely potent. Acts of kindness in their memory, helping the poor with a loan, or helping a bride and groom with their wedding expenses are all great ways of helping the deceased," I continued.

"Yes," Anna said, "I can commit to some of these."

"It's ironic, Anna, that most of the things people do for the dead these days are associated with the body: making a nice funeral, preparing a nice casket, etc. But helping the soul on its arduous journey is something they really don't even think about," I shared, hoping the impact of this emotional heart-wrenching day would help my friend Morris find peace in Heaven and that his shaken family left behind would find peace here on earth.

Continuation:
Coping With Grief By Making
a Living Legacy

It was exactly one year to the day after Morris's passing. Jerry had invited some of his close friends to join him at his home as he marked this solemn milestone, the first *yahrtzeit*. Jerry asked me to join them, and also to share what had transpired the previous month on our trip to Poland. All of us were still shaken up from the revelations of that trip and were still having a hard time coming to terms with Morris's past.

Overall, looking back at the year, it had been quite a challenging one, with all the colorful conversations, revelations, trips, and debates that had transpired. But despite all the ups and downs, I finally felt, as the year came to an end, a feeling of inner peace and satisfaction.

In my mind, I had made some major inroads with Jerry. Being entrusted by my hero Morris to bring back his one and only son Jerry from the clutches of atheism and extreme secularism was quite a daunting task. I can't say that I had succeeded influencing him toward becoming very devout, yet I believe that I had at least helped to soften his world outlook. Even his mother, Anna, had warmed up to some of the spiritual ideas we had spoken about over the course of the past year.

Thinking about Anna, there was still something about her that I needed to understand. Lots of new information had been revealed in Poland about Morris, in addition to the revelations about his stint as a Sonderkommando. Yet Anna still remained a mystery. With all that I had found out about Morris, I felt compelled to ask Anna some questions about her past—how she had survived war-torn Europe. I hoped I would have a chance to speak to her before Jerry's friends came.

I arrived a little early to offer emotional support and to make sure I had what I needed for my speech and for the rest of the program. Anna approached me in the kitchen, offering me a tea. This was my chance to speak to her, and I grabbed it.

"Anna, you never told me much about your past, other than the fact that you came from Lodz, like Morris. Who were your parents, Anna?" I asked boldly, as she poured the hot water into the elegant porcelain cup.

"What is this, some kind of an interview, Rabbi?" asked Anna, suspicious. Her reaction was nothing unusual for a Holocaust survivor, who, by nature, hate interrogations. I think she was also suspicious because of our discoveries of her husband's past.

"I was just curious, that's all," I said gently. I didn't want to upset her.

"Serious? You want to hear about my parents, Rabbi?" Anna asked in a light tone. "How much time have you got?"

"Anna, to hear your story I will make the time," I said, glancing at my notes quickly before she began, so I could give her my undivided attention.

"It's a pity you never met my parents. I know you would have liked them. My parents were extremely pious people. They were your type," she said with a sly smile.

"My type? What do you mean by that?" I asked, growing more and more curious about Anna's roots.

"You could call them religious people," Anna began. "They ran an inn on Piotrkowska Street in Lodz, Poland—something like a bed and breakfast. Everyone in town knew them as the most hospitable and kind people you could ever meet. Anyone down and out, who needed a place to stay, could always count on my parents."

"So, let me ask you a personal question, Anna," I interrupted, not wanting to lose the chance I had always been waiting for. "If your parents were religious Jews, like you say, how is it that you gave it all up? Especially since your husband was very much the traditional type?"

"*Oy*, Rabbi, why do you ask me these hurtful questions when you know the answers very well?" she said, sounding impatient and annoyed. "What do you expect from me after living through what I did?"

I nodded sympathetically, and was prepared to shift the conversation. Surprisingly, she continued to open up.

"Where was G–d when they led my parents to the gas chambers? And how about my little sister, who was murdered by those Nazi beasts?" Anna choked back tears. "And then they took away my older sister, my beautiful sister of twenty-one years. Until this day, we have no idea where she disappeared to. Can you imagine living through such atrocities?"

I shook my head now. How could I possibly understand? I could empathize, and I had many family members who had a similar background to Anna and Morris. But I was not a survivor myself. Before I could respond, Anna continued talking.

"Rabbi, of course I would have loved to continue my parents' traditions, but the Nazis killed my soul, Rabbi. They robbed me of my humanity. Not a night goes by that I don't dream of my family. My father and mother were such decent people, true role models to the community," she said, holding back sobs.

I really felt bad for opening up this can of worms with Jerry's mother, but it was too late to stop. Anna kept talking.

"Do you know that my older sister…she was so beautiful with gorgeous blonde hair and blue eyes like mine. She was a real catch. From when she was sixteen years old, all the matchmakers in town would line up at my parents' door to present offers of the finest young boys in town. And then she disappeared, just like that, poof," Anna said angrily.

"Tell me Anna, I am interested to know more about this older sister. Did you ever try locating her after the war?" I wondered if finding her sister was possible. Maybe she hadn't died, like the rest of her family. Especially with Morris gone, Anna needed the comfort and connection of family.

"No one survived! You know that, Rabbi," Anna said strongly. "Obviously, I looked high and low after the war, to the best of my ability, but to no avail. Rabbi, everyone knows what that means. Hitler killed them all!" she said with despair.

"But tell me, Anna," I pressed. Something inside of me drove me to continue pursuing the possibility that Anna's sister survived. Something sounded odd about the story, like there was a missing piece we didn't know yet.

"What was this beautiful sister's name?" I asked her.

"My sister's name? What's the difference to you?"

"Just curiosity, again," I told her, but it was more than that.

"Chaya was her name," Anna said, looking down at the floor.

I suddenly became cold. A chill went up my spine. Something was very familiar here, too familiar.

"Was her full name Chaya Breindel, perhaps? I asked slowly. Anna looked at me with her small eyes wide with amazement.

"Yes, how did you guess that Rabbi?" Anna asked, incredulous.

"I don't know how to say this, but that was my grandmother's name. Everything you said to describe her was so accurate. The blonde hair, the sisters, the parent's bed and breakfast on Piotrkowska Street in Lodz, all of this is exactly as my grandmother described it," I shared.

"Chaya Breindel? My older sister? Alive?" Anna said in a whisper. "This can't be true! I thought she was dead, surely she was killed by Hitler!"

"I knew my grandmother so well. I just know it's her. Many nights she would sit with me as a young boy and tell me stories about her life in Poland, specifically about her younger sister Chana. I guess that must be your Yiddish name." I looked toward Anna warmly. She was shaking, and tears were pouring down her cheeks.

"I just can't believe it. After all these years, Morris was my great uncle and you are my great aunt," I exclaimed, unsure how Anna would react to this news. Sometimes, I feared she didn't appreciate Morris's participation in the synagogue.

"We are family, for sure!" Anna said in disbelief.

"I can't believe that my dear grandmother, whom I loved so much, was your sister. What a pity she passed away ten years ago in New York, and never had a chance to see you," I said. Now tears were threatening to come down my cheeks. Anna was my aunt, and she accepted our familial connections.

"I guess that my strong connection to your family was not just by choice, Anna. It was something very deep, like my genetics were attracting me to your family all along," I said in wonder. This was so unexpected.

I could see that Anna was also stunned. She was in another space. Not just because she discovered that her sister she wrote off as dead was alive for all those years, but also because her whole life was now in turmoil. Many of her life choices were based on the assumption that her sister had died. Had she known otherwise, perhaps, who knows what would be different.

Jerry walked into the kitchen, and witnessed his mother and me crying. "What's going on?" Jerry said. "Why is my mother crying?"

"Jerry, my son, you won't believe it. I just found out that we're related to the rabbi," Anna said, through tears.

"What?" Jerry asked, confused.

'My grandmother was your mother's older sister," I

answered, wiping my tears with a crumpled tissue I found in my pocket. "Your aunt, Chaya Breindel, wasn't lost at Auschwitz. She made it to New York, where she raised a family—my family! In short, we're cousins."

Jerry stooped down and went dead silent. I don't know if it was because of the revelation about his long-lost aunt who wasn't so lost anymore, or it was the shock of being related all along to his father's rabbi whom he'd previously ignored for the longest time.

After a long lapse of time, he straightened out and said:

"Wow, Rabbi. I can't believe this! First, my father is a collaborator, and now my mother is related to you. So what does that make us?" Jerry half-chuckled in middle of this mad revelation.

"Who cares, Jerry, maybe second cousins, or something like that. The bottom line is that, all along, I felt this inexplicable connection to your family, and now I know why," I said, feeling joyful.

"So we were in on this together, Rabbi, more than we ever knew. All these years of your friendship and rabbinical services for my father, and you were his nephew all along," Jerry said, as he processed this new information.

"I can't believe it myself," I told Anna and Jerry. "It explains why I felt so close to Morris and to your family."

"All this time that you were trying to comfort our family, and it was your own personal loss as well! Then for the zinger: On what day do we discover all these fantastic revelations? On the one-year anniversary of my father's passing," Jerry noted. "Wow!"

Jerry patted me warmly on the back. Anna smiled, looking content.

We sat for several moments in silence, digesting what had just transpired. Jerry's wife, Lisa, came into the kitchen to check on all of us and to get help with setting up for the event. Jerry spoke first, sharing the news of our familial ties with his wife, who was thrilled.

"I always thought you were like a brother to Jerry," said his wife, beckoning Anna to come and help with the centerpieces.

Once the women left, Jerry turned to me and said, "Rabbi, my head is hurting me from all these new family revelations. But until we internalize this, maybe I can confide in you—as both my relative and my rabbi—that something is hurting me today on the first anniversary of my father's death. Life is just not the same without my dad. While you have comforted me greatly over the last year with our deep discussions about how his soul lives on forever in Heaven, and how we can even communicate with him occasionally, I still need him down here at my side, badly," Jerry shared. He looked sad. "I didn't appreciate him enough when he was alive."

"Your father is with you, Jerry. He remains in your heart. People that we love always remain in our hearts," I told him. Yet my words felt inadequate: I knew that having someone in your heart feels much, much farther away than sitting across from them at the kitchen table.

"It's not the same, Rabbi," Jerry said with sadness. "Just not the same."

"You're right, Jerry," I echoed. "It's different. This reminds me of a story about the Rebbe and his wife."

"Go ahead, Rabbi," Jerry urged me on. "I still can't figure out how you know so many stories."

"Rabbi School," I said with a chuckle, hoping that a story would lighten Jerry's mood.

> There was once a plumber visiting my Rebbe's home in the very Chassidic area of Crown Heights, in Brooklyn, New York. Unaware that he was in the home of not-just-another rabbi, the plumber told the Rebbe's wife, "I noticed that in every home in this neighborhood, there is always a big picture of the Chief

Rebbe in the dining room. Why don't you have one? Are you perhaps not so Chassidic?"

The Rebbe's wife responded, "Others hang their Rebbe's picture on the wall, while I carry him in my heart!"

"Cute story, Rabbi, but that's still a little too airy-fairy for me. While I do believe that my father lives on in my heart, I still want to hold onto his hand, and feel his physical presence," Jerry mourned.

"In addition to your father being present in spirit, in your heart, there actually is a physical aspect of your father here on earth, just waiting for you to connect to it," I reassured.

"Sure, Rabbi" said Jerry speaking in a cynical sing-song." I'm sure there is a physical part of Dad still here. His poor body's disintegrating in the earth as we speak. Nah, that's not much of a comfort for me, Rabbi."

"Obviously I'm not referring to that! I'm speaking about an actual organic, physical part of your father that lives on in this world and is very much alive and well, making a significant difference here on earth even after his death," I continued.

"What are you talking about, Rabbi?" Jerry said. "I'm not following. I certainly don't see him."

"But neither did your mother see her sister Chaya, who was alive and well for so many years in New York after the Holocaust!" I could not help but use the newly revealed information to make my point.

"The world is a complicated place with many layers of existence. We may not see everything in front of our eyes. Sometimes we may mistake someone as dead because we don't see the full picture!"

"But what's the comparison? My aunt Chaya was alive, though unknown to us, and my father is dead, Rabbi!"

"No, Jerry, your father remains alive in his good deeds, Jerry," I said, trying to clarify.

"How is that? Deeds are not alive either!" Jerry protested.

"The Jewish mystics write that good people live on in this world—even after their death and in an even greater measure than when they were alive in the conventional sense—through their good deeds," I told him.

"But how is that possible, Rabbi? Even the best people are buried, and their souls return to Heaven? If my memory serves me right, I am pretty sure that you said that all of our good deeds escort us to Heaven, leaving nothing of value behind?" Jerry challenged.

"True, but not exactly true, Jerry," I said, wondering how to explain this complex topic.

"Now I am really not sure I get what you're saying," Jerry said, looking bewildered.

"While the spiritual effects of our good deeds follow us on our journey to Heaven, our physical achievements remain down here on earth. They become a living force of nature—unstoppable and vibrant. All of our important contributions in refining and correcting this world actually remain in the physical realm. Even after we die and are unable to continue performing good deeds, we still leave behind an indelible impression that lives on. This is our unique, individual living legacy that becomes an integral part of the collective human "imprint" on this physical world," I explained. I took a sip of the tea Anna had made me an hour before. It was cold, yet soothing.

"This needs a story," Jerry said, joking.

"OK: here you go," I said, hoping this tale would make him laugh.

A visitor to Israel attended a recital and concert at the Moscovitz Auditorium. He was quite impressed with the architecture and the acoustics. He inquired of the tour guide, "Is this magnificent auditorium named after Chaim Moscovitz, the famous Talmudic scholar?"

"No," replied the guide. "It is named after Sam Moscovitz, the writer."

"I never heard of him. What did he write?"

"A check," replied the guide.

"I like that—an imprint on the physical world is our living legacy," Jerry reflected. "I was actually wondering: If Heaven is as spectacular a place as you said it is—a world of truth, proper perspective, and no suffering—why do we spend so much time in *this* world, experiencing so many hardships and challenges, only to return back, with all our achievements, to the place where it all started? Seems circular and futile to me."

"There must be something very worthwhile in experiencing this physical world, and something that we need to accomplish *here*, by making a difference in *this* world," I added.

"But, Rabbi, I am getting mixed messages from you. Is it ultimately this world, or the next world where our actions really count?" Jerry questioned.

"Jerry, that's a great question. Chapter five of *Ethics of the Fathers*, also known as *Pirkei Avot*, from the Talmud, speaks precisely about the same paradox."

> Rabbi Yaakov would say: This world is comparable to the antechamber before the World to Come. Prepare yourself in the antechamber, so that you may enter the banquet hall.
>
> He would also say: A single moment of repentance and good deeds in this world is greater than all of the World to Come. And a single moment of bliss in the World to Come is greater than all of the present world.

"That's cryptic, Rabbi," Jerry commented.

"At first glance, it would appear that Rabbi Yaakov is speaking from both sides of his mouth. First he says the next world is greater, and then, in the same breath, he says that this world is greater. Which is truly greater: The sweet bliss in store for us in Heaven, in the afterlife? Or the good deeds performed in *this* world?" I summarized the conundrum.

"So, what's the solution? Jerry mused.

"In classical rabbinic tradition, it all depends on what you're looking for. If you're a pleasure seeker, and I'm talking about real pleasure here, not the temporary physical fleeting pleasure of the body, but the more permanent stress-free spiritual pleasure that comes from the clarity and tranquility of the soul. That can be found mostly in Heaven, not on earth. Heaven is where the angels enjoy the sweetest nectar of the Divine fruit. But if what you're looking for is to make a real difference with your existence, *that*, believe it or not, happens down here on earth, when we perform good deeds—acts of charity and kindness," I told him. "When we help a poor person, when we visit the sick, when we build a synagogue or educate a child, we are making a difference, and this world is where it counts."

"That's beautiful, Rabbi," Jerry said. "So our actions here *do* matter."

"Yes, It's here, down on earth where your father Morris made a difference with his charitable acts of kindness, and where he left an everlasting impression and 'imprint,' through his good deeds," I said, missing Morris more than ever.

> In a Sunday school class, a teacher asked the children, "How many of you would like to go to Heaven?" All hands went up, except the hand of one little boy.
>
> The teacher then asked, "And how many of you would like to go to the other place?" Not one hand went up.
>
> So the teacher turned to the little boy who didn't raise his hand in answer to either of the questions and said to him, "Jackie, don't you want to go anywhere?"
>
> "No," replied the boy, "I like it right here!"

"But Rabbi, how can this awful world of confusion serve a higher purpose? Sounds like a contradiction in terms to me," Jerry said passionately.

"It's precisely the lowliness of this world that serves as a dramatic backdrop to contrast with our good deeds, to highlight their true value," I explained. "Back in Heaven, in the world of goodness and perfection, there's no real appreciation of good things. Goodness is taken for granted. It *is* Heaven, after all! Only in an evil world like ours, where there is so much temptation and sin, can goodness be truly appreciated. It's only in a place where goodness is the oddball, that it can be truly and effectively contrasted."

"OK, so we can appreciate the good here, whereas in Heaven, good deeds are the norm," Jerry summed up.

"And that's the purpose of our existence on earth—to bring a little light into this place of darkness in all of our daily struggles," I said, smiling.

"But, Rabbi, if I get you right, the only benefit of this world is that it serves as a backdrop for our good deeds. Are you implying that there's no redeeming quality to the world itself?" Jerry asked.

"Deep question, Jerry," I responded. "There's a concept in Kabbalah that claims that there is great value and holiness invested in the physical world itself, waiting to be uncovered and released by us humans."

"How does that happen?" Jerry prodded.

"The Kabbalah teaches that there are dormant sparks of holiness, originating from the highest order, that get lost in the physical world and need to be extricated, reactivated, and restored by us—almost like a genie trapped in a bottle," I said, hoping to elucidate this spiritual concept.

Jerry chuckled at my genie reference and motioned for me to continue.

"When we successfully release and reactivate these 'sparks,' we gain personally from the power unleashed in the process. But more importantly, by restoring these sparks to their source, we bring about perfection in the cosmos," I said. "This mystical concept is connected to bringing redemption to the world. When we succeed in releasing the last of these hidden, holy sparks, we will bring the Moshiach [the Messiah, in Hebrew]," I exclaimed.

"Do we really believe in Moshiach?" Jerry said cynically. "It sounds so unrealistic that a charismatic leader will just fly down from Heaven and bring world peace."

"Well, the Kabbalah views the Moshiach as the culmination of a spiritual process from the beginning of time, bringing spiritual perfection to the world through *tikkun olam*—fixing the world and perfecting it," I told him.

"I like that—*tikkun olam*," Jerry repeated.

"Every time we do acts of goodness, we release some of these sparks and redeem them. Only after we will succeed in releasing all of the sparks, will we usher in a new era in which the Moshiach can arrive," I expounded.

"It's hard to imagine such an era," Jerry said, looking into the distance. In the silent moment, noises of the *yahrtzeit* preparation filtered into the kitchen. "What will it be like?"

"The messianic era will be a time when we will see all that was accomplished in the physical world—the accomplishments of every soul that ever walked the earth, in every generation, will be recognized in the physical world," I shared. "All of your father's beautiful deeds will become evident to all!"

Jerry nodded in his familiar way, urging me to continue talking.

"This physical world is not just a stepping stone to Heaven. Rather, it is actually the goal itself. The changes and improvements we make to this world—our imprints—endure forever. They are parts of us that remain down here on earth, even after we've completed our individual personal journey," I said, thinking about what my own contributions would be.

"That's really heavy stuff, Rabbi, but it still doesn't cut it for me. I need my father, the person, here on earth: not just his enduring legacy of good deeds embedded in the fabric of the world," Jerry challenged. I sensed the depths of his longing for his father.

"It's not merely his legacy and his imprint on the physical world that remain. There is an actual physical part of your father too," I told him.

"How's that, Rabbi?" Jerry asked in wonder.

"You, Jerry, and your progeny are your father's enduring physical continuation in this world. There is an actual physical piece of your father's living DNA that remains in this world through you," I explained.

"That's a bit far-fetched, no?" Jerry argued.

"This is a very ancient Jewish idea based on a mysterious tradition recorded in the Talmud. Jacob, the third of the Jewish patriarchs, who lived around the year 1500 BCE, never really died. You see, while the deaths of the first two patriarchs of the Jewish people, Jacob's father Isaac and his grandfather Abraham, are clearly recorded in the Bible, there is, mysteriously, no record of the death of third patriarch, Jacob. Hence, the legend says that Jacob never died and continues living to this very day," I shared.

"Uh huh," Jerry said skeptically. "Doesn't sound too Jewish to me. This idea sounds more like a Christian idea."

"The Talmud points out the Bible does not mention Jacob's actual death, yet it does record his burial, the eulogies at his funeral, and even his being embalmed," I explained.

"So, if Jacob were alive, would they have buried, eulogized, and embalmed a living person?" Jerry asked.

"The Talmud answers that because Jacob's children were alive, he was considered alive. Jacob's death was intentionally omitted from the Bible because Jacob was considered virtually alive, even in his buried state. Since all of Jacob's children remained faithful to the moral path that he'd taught them (in contrast with some of his ancestors' children who rejected their parents' path), Jacob was considered as if he'd never died. His children are his living legacy," I explained.

"So you're saying that Jacob's soul may have gone to Heaven, and his body may have been interred in the earth, but he was never considered dead because his physical presence was still very much alive through his children, who continued in his life path here on earth," Jerry reiterated as he processed the concept. He folded his arms and leaned against the counter.

"Jerry, I don't know if you ever heard the story of the three buddies," I said.

"Try me, Rabbi," Jerry said. "I enjoy your stories."

Dovid, Shlomo, and Yaakov died in a car crash. But they were good Jews, so they went to Heaven, they were ushered right into Heaven's orientation process.

They were each asked, "When you are in your casket, and friends and family are mourning you, what would you like to hear them say about you?"

Dovid says, "I would like to hear them say that I was great among the doctors my time and that I was a great family man."

Shlomo says, "I would like to hear that I was a wonderful husband and school teacher, who made a difference for our children of tomorrow."

Yaakov replies, "I would like to hear them say…'LOOK, LOOK! HE'S MOVING!!!'"

Jerry laughed heartily at the corny story.

"By the way, did you ever notice the writing on a Jewish tombstone?" I asked him, changing the topic.

"Sure, Rabbi," Jerry answered. "We took a lot of time thinking about what to write on my father's headstone."

"Did you ever notice an unusual abbreviation or acrostic at the bottom of it?" I pressed.

"You mean R.I.P.?" Jerry said quizzically.

"No, Jerry. That's 'Rest in Peace.' I'm speaking about the standard Hebrew inscription written on every Jewish stone in the cemetery."

"Oh that? I remember seeing it. It's some five Hebrew letters," Jerry answered.

"Yes, Jerry, they appear as:

תנצב"ה

It's an acrostic that stands for 'May the soul be tied in the bond of life.' Why the 'bond of life'?" I put the question to Jerry.

"I have no idea, Rabbi," Jerry said. "It seems like it would say something about the afterlife at the cemetery."

The answer is that when we say the "bond of life," we are speaking about a tangible bond with the living: the living legacy, our children. You see, no person can be replaced. An individual soul is too large, infinite, and unquantifiable. Every person is unique and one of a kind. When they die, they leave behind an irreplaceable void," I told him.

"It sure does feel that way," Jerry affirmed.

"One comfort to the family is the knowledge that each child replaces a small facet of their parent's legacy. The sum total of all their children's contributions to improve this world collectively replaces the devastating emptiness left behind," I explained. "But this can happen only when the children join together to replenish the loss. Only when they're bonded to each other!"

"Good thing I'm an only child," Jerry quipped.

"Yes, because if they choose to fight and squabble amongst themselves, as is often the case, there's no meaningful continuity. Only when they join hands, the children and grandchildren together, can they successfully keep their parent's legacy alive. Because every descendant individually reflects minimal aspects of the DNA, together they can project the complete presence of their deceased parent in this world," I clarified. Jerry's kids were part of Morris's legacy, too.

"Rabbi, I love what you are saying, but I still miss my father's physical presence on earth. All your ideas about his children and his good deeds still fall short of actually having the man alive and in the physical world," Jerry said.

Since I had failed to offer comfort with my words, I put my arm around him in a bear hug, and pulled out a classic line from my rabbinical hat. It's what rabbis typically remember when all else fails: "Jerry, not to worry about holding your father again, as you'll surely be reunited with him once again very soon."

"Huh?" said Jerry, opening his eyes incredulously. "Did I hear you correctly? Are you sending me off to Heaven before my time, to go and reunite with my father?"

"No, never Jerry! I am surely not sending you anywhere. You are too dear to me, Jerry. And besides, we were speaking about holding your father in the physical realm, not in Heaven."

Jerry looked relieved. "What did you mean, then?"

"I am referring to your father's eventual physical return to reunite with you at the resurrection of the dead," I said, wondering how he would react.

"Rabbi, that is even more absurd than what I suggested. Are you telling me that you actually believe in the dead coming back to life? I know we spoke about this before, but do you truly believe that my dead father will return like that?" Jerry said dismissively. "That sounds ridiculous to me."

"Yes, Jerry, on the surface it may sound ridiculous, but let me share a personal conversation I had with your father in the hospital," I said, hoping this was the right path, one that would help Jerry heal. "While lying on his deathbed, very sick and a bit delirious, just hours before he died, he began telling me this, out of the blue."

"What did he say already?" Jerry said impatiently.

"Rabbi," he said, "you know how much I love the theatre, and how much I enjoyed taking my wife to a nice play. Well, in my view, Rabbi, I view all of life as a long extended play. To me, it is an ongoing play that continues not just the span of one lifetime, but over the course of many generations. Every generation is like another scene with new actors."

"Rabbi," your father said. "I am very sick, and I believe that my part in this play is coming to an end shortly. I have done my best to play my part with gusto, to the best of my ability. But now my scene is coming to a close, and the new actors must take over."

"Rabbi, I need you to find the right time and the right words to explain to my son Jerry that he needs to take over my part and continue our family story and the ongoing narrative of the Jewish people. Tell him that I know that he will feel lonely at times without us actors of the earlier scenes, but that we will be sitting backstage together with his grandparents, all the way back to the Jewish patriarchs, Abraham, Isaac, and Jacob, cheering him on, and encouraging him to do his part."

"Tell him not to worry, because at the very end, when they finally close the curtain on this play, after the final scene, all the old actors will come out to take a final bow together. Tell him that we will be reunited once again," I recounted, watching Jerry carefully for his reaction.

"Rabbi, my father really said that? How profound and hopeful. What a beautiful, poetic way of viewing life, and the continuity of the generations, as part of an ongoing story that continues to unfold. I didn't know my dad had such a poetic side to him," Jerry said with wonder.

"Those were your father's words not mine," I reassured. "He told me, "Make no mistake. We will be reunited once again.""

"I really like it Rabbi, but this last part about coming back and taking a bow doesn't sit well with me. Why the need for the soul to *shlep* back to this wretched world to return in a body?

Why can't the souls in Heaven simply enjoy the 'play' and just take a bow up there?" Jerry challenged.

"The return of the body to this world is essential to the afterlife. Contrary to the popular notion that the ultimate existence and final destination of the soul is the extraterrestrial life in Heaven, the Kabbalah maintains that perfection will be achieved here in the physical world at the end of times," I explained.

"That's counterintuitive," Jerry pointed out, motioning for me to delve deeper.

"On the cosmic level, we're taught that there's something profound and lofty concealed in the physical stuff that makes up this world. Likewise, on the micro level, there's great genius and divinity to be found in the individual physical body. The body is not just a utilitarian tool the soul uses to fulfill its mission in this world; rather, it's an equal partner with the soul. Both body and soul are essential in successfully fulfilling a common mission and purpose. In fact, in some ways, the body shares a deeper relationship with G–d, surpassing the Divine soul," I said, hoping to offer some clarity.

"How could that be true?" Jerry asked.

"Obviously, with all the vices and stigmas associated with the physical body, it is hard for us to discern the body's greatness today. Its true status will be revealed only in the era of the resurrection of the dead, when the body will reunite with the soul in its perfect form. At that time, instead of the body and soul competing with each other, they will be totally aligned and fused into one integrated being with a common goal. When that occurs, the soul will not only align with the body, but it will draw great spiritual sustenance from the body, whose source — according to the Kabbalah — surpasses even the soul's. Together they will reveal the perfection of humanity that we have been working on from the beginning of time, and from then on, body and soul will live in unity happily ever after."

"That's wild," Jerry commented. "Hard to imagine what that would be like."

This was precisely what your father understood. This is where the play takes place! This is the stage! Planet earth! This was your father's last directive to you, Jerry," I said passionately. I pictured Morris in those last days, making spiritual connections and pronouncements from his hospital bed.

Jerry was moved by his father's last directive and was processing and internalizing it. He closed his eyes for a few moments, concentrating deeply, and then he reopened them. I saw a new light in his eyes. It looked like he had made an important discovery.

"Rabbi," Jerry began. "Let me share a brainstorm after all the meaningful conversations we've had about the afterlife, and especially after this last directive from my father. In all of our conversations, especially today's, you've made it abundantly clear that the best place to connect with my father is right here in this physical world, and not in Heaven. I feel that I need to do something to connect with my father, just like you said, right here in this physical world. Yes: as his one and only son, I feel my duty to leave his imprint on the physical landscape. I want to make a meaningful and tangible legacy from my father," Jerry proclaimed.

"Wow, that's inspiring, Jerry," I encouraged.

"Brace yourself, Rabbi. This is all about your good friend and great uncle Morris," Jerry said with a smile.

"Sure, Jerry!" I answered, on the edge of my seat about what he would say.

"So, in keeping with what we discussed, I must tell you that I couldn't help but notice that my father's greatest pride and joy—his beloved synagogue—is in a state of disrepair. It has become an eyesore in the community. I would like to do something to turn this important house of worship into a majestic building that my father would be proud of, by replacing the old crumbling synagogue with a brand new one in his memory," Jerry said. "That's what I would like to do, Rabbi."

"Are you serious, Jerry?" I stood there totally flabbergasted.

"I want you to find the best architects, engineers, and decorators that money can buy, and make this synagogue of yours a world-class building," Jerry said, waving his arm in a dramatic flourish.

"I have no words, Jerry," I told him. "Thank you. Your father would be very proud."

The doorbell rang with guests for the *yahrtzeit* observance. Jerry and I left the kitchen and walked into the elegant dining room, where refreshments had been set up. Jerry went to shake hands with his friends who had come to support him as his year of mourning ended.

I stood waiting for my turn to speak at the event, reflecting over the year I'd spent with Jerry. Mostly, I was stunned, not because of the financial windfall bestowed upon our community, or because of the badly-needed renovations that our decrepit synagogue was about to receive. Mainly, I was awestruck by the wisdom of my mentor Morris. Here I was, witnessing the incredible influence that my deceased friend and uncle, Morris, exercised from on high—and not only over his son. Morris even managed—from Heaven—to successfully transform our community, making an indelible imprint on the physical world!

Epilogue

One year later, I found myself standing with my wife and children outside our new synagogue building. It was a beautiful day: the sun was out in its glory. Jerry pulled up in his limousine with his own family: his mother, Anna, his wife, Lisa, his children, his granddaughter Jordana, and the new grandchildren, Morris and Jesse, dressed in their finest clothing for the occasion.

The entire congregation was seated in a massive tent constructed on the new beautiful landscaped garden that adorned the stunning new building. Everyone who was a "somebody" in our synagogue was in attendance. The rabbinical council of Ottawa was well represented, and even the hip Rabbi Cohen from the next township came. I looked around and saw Avraham Eisen, the tour guide from Israel, who had ironically become very close to Jerry since that fateful trip to Auschwitz. Jerry must have flown him in for the occasion. Even Jerry's hardheaded childhood friend, Jack Rabinowitz, was there too!

I knew that Jerry was a man of his word, but this building was just spectacular. Its scope was beyond my wildest dreams. It was a state-of-the-art building with a newly added center for youth that was one of its kind in the world and became the talk of the town overnight!

Jerry came to join me on the stage. I handed him the mike.

"Just over two years ago, I buried my father. My father and I did not see eye to eye for many years. Along with the conflicts I'd had with him over the last few years of his life, there was an ongoing spiritual rift that had developed between the two of us, going back for as long as I can remember. We found ourselves at two opposite ends of the spiritual spectrum. I could never appreciate his love for his synagogue and religion, nor could he appreciate my love for what I would call the finer things of this material world," Jerry said, choking back tears.

"But over the last year, something changed. Attempting to come to terms with the loss of my father, and dealing with my guilt and need for reconciliation, I discovered that I have an innate desire to continue where my father left off—to complete that which he'd started.

In the words of my beloved father, "Life is a long, extended theatrical play." Every generation brings a new scene with new actors, continuing the story."

There was a flutter of applause from the audience.

"It gives me great honor to be a part of this unfolding story that features unbelievable actors like my father! I found out, over the course of my year of mourning for my father—with the guidance of Rabbi G., who also happens to be my newfound cousin—that there are many meaningful ways to reconnect with my father and perpetuate his legacy," Jerry continued.

"I learned to let go of my anger and to offload the burden of guilt and resentment I harbored toward my father, first by asking my father for forgiveness and then later by offering him forgiveness."

Tears flowed among the listeners as Jerry shared his healing process, how he processed his grief.

"Finally I can live with myself and move ahead with a positive relationship with my father. A little over a year ago I visited Auschwitz, the largest Jewish cemetery in the world, where 1.1 million Jews were murdered in cold blood. There I discovered what my father went through to survive. While I was initially disappointed with some of my father's choices, with time,

I realized how his choices ensured survival, ultimately giving me the gift of life."

At this point, Jerry paused again as the audience applauded in support of his words.

"In return, I made a commitment to give back to my father by continuing his journey in this world. Ladies and gentlemen, it gives me great honor to dedicate this new building. It was a dream of my father to rebuild the synagogue he loved so much and to help Rabbi G., my good friend and relative." He looked at me and smiled warmly.

"I am grateful that G–d gave me the means to share with this community and to make an eternal legacy for my father," Jerry said, turning his attention to the stone on the stage next to him.

We unveiled the foundation stone, which said:

In loving memory of Morris Goldstein,
donated by his son, Jerry

The entire congregation erupted in applause. People stood to honor and congratulate both Jerry and me. As Jerry and I moved toward the new building, surrounded by Morris's community and Jerry's friends, Jerry tapped me on the shoulder, and whispered, "Thank you for giving me back my father!"

Jerry's Questions

Compiled here is a list of the questions discussed throughout the book, for review and group discussions.

Conversation 1: The Soul

- What is the proof that a human soul exists?
- Is the soul a spiritual entity, or some fine physical energy like electricity?
- Maybe there is no soul and it is strictly the brain that calls the shots?
- If we are scientific people, how can we believe in an "invisible" soul?
- If the body expires, why doesn't the soul expire too?
- What is the soul? What is its function?
- If they both trace their roots to the Divine, what is the difference between body and soul?
- Since it is so elusive, how can we experience the soul?

Conversation 2: Personality

- Do souls keep their personality and their cherished relationships in the afterlife?
- Do souls arrive with a predefined personality, or is it only the physical DNA and life experiences that are responsible for our personality?
- If all souls are from a singular Divine source, how do we account for diverse personalities?
- What is the connection between the personality and the name given?

- How can parents identify and select the correct (personality) name for their child?
- In the afterlife, will the soul graduate and forget its earthly personality?
- How can we recognize a soul in the afterlife without a physical body?
- Do family bonds remain intact in the afterlife? Do parents and children — or soul mates — remain connected forever?
- Do memories and a sense of nostalgia remain in the afterlife?
- Do souls carry grudges into the next world?

Conversation 3: Heaven

- Is there a proof for the existence of Heaven?
- How can we enjoy Heaven without bodies?
- What is Heaven, really?
- Is there a grand tribunal when we arrive in Heaven, that judges us arbitrarily?
- Do Jews believe in Hell? In devils with pitchforks?
- Shouldn't a G–d be beyond imposing punishment in the afterlife? Isn't that a form of vindictiveness?

Conversation 4: Suffering

- Why do bad things happen to good people? Why do they suffer?
- Do we believe in suffering for the sins of others?
- Can we suffer for the sins of our parents?
- Do we believe in suffering for the sins of a previous incarnation of the soul?

- Do Jews believe in reincarnation?
- Does suffering in this world spare us from suffering in the World to Come?
- Is it OK to question or challenge G–d?
- How does one continue to pray or observe religion after being subjected to suffering?

Conversation 5: Communicating

- Can we communicate with the dead?
- Is the soul more present and accessible at the cemetery than anywhere else?
- How can the gravesite serve as a portal for the soul if all that is left is decomposed remains?
- Can a modern person educated in science believe in a resurrection of the dead?
- Isn't praying at the cemetery to a dead person a form of idolatry or cult practice?
- Can we speak to the dead if we left off with them on bad terms?
- How do we ask forgiveness from someone who is dead?
- Besides visiting the grave, are there any other ways to reach out to the dead?
- Why do the mystics disallow giving away the shoes of the deceased?

Conversation 6: Helping

- Does the soul suffer in its transition to the afterlife?
- Is the soul traumatized by leaving its family?
- What can we do to help the soul in its transition?

- Why doesn't the Jewish memorial prayer, Kaddish, make any mention of death?
- Why do Jews wash their hands when leaving the cemetery?
- Can we say a memorial prayer for a sinner or, even worse, a criminal or an abuser?

Conversation 7: Legacy

- How can we hold on to our deceased loved ones down here on earth?
- In the scheme of things, is it this world or the World to Come that is most important?
- What possible benefit to the spiritual soul can come from engaging in this lowly physical world?
- What is the Jewish concept of "Moshiach"?
- Do all departed souls return in a physical body at some point? For what purpose?

Conversation 1: *Likkutei Amarim — Tanya* ("*Tanya*"), by Rabbi Schneur Zalman of Liadi, ch. 2

Conversation 2: *Tanya*, ibid., ch. 3

Conversation 3: *Tanya*, ibid., ch. 8

Conversation 4: *Tanya*, ibid., ch. 26; writings and talks of the Rebbe, Rabbi Menachem Mendel Schneerson, the seventh Lubavitcher Rebbe

Conversation 5: *Kuntres HaHishtatchus*, by Rabbi Dovber of Lubavitch, the "Mitteler Rebbe"

Conversation 6: Talmud, Sanhedrin 104a

Conversation 7: *Pirkei Avot*, ch. 4; Talmud, Ta'anis 5b

Chevra Kadisha
  The Jewish burial society.

Kabbalah
  Jewish mysticism.

Kaddish
  Famous Jewish prayer recited to honour the dead.

Kiddush
  Ceremony of prayer and blessing over wine at the Sabbath
  and holiday meals.

Seder
  The traditional Passover evening meal.

Talmud
  The authoritative record of the oral tradition of Judaism
  and famous repository of Jewish wisdom.

Torah
  The five books of Moses but more generally refers to the
  entire body of Jewish teaching.

Tzaddik
  A righteous person

Yahrtzeit
  The memorial anniversary of the date of death.

Yizkor
  The memorial prayer recited on major Jewish holidays.

Acknowledgments

I would like to thank, at this time, the following great people who have made this book possible:

- The Lubavitcher Rebbe, my teacher, who inspired me to spend my entire life helping others and paying attention to their spiritual and physical well-being;
- Rabbis Manis Friedman, YY Jacobson, Simon Jacobson, and Aron Moss, for some of the ideas shared;
- Yedida Wolfe, for helping develop the storyline and for editing;
- Ya'akovah Weber, for proofreading and copy editing;
- Steeles Memorial Chapel, of Toronto, for their sponsorship;
- The members of my great community at Chabad of Markham, who have given me the opportunity to teach and counsel for the last thirty-five years;
- My dear wife, Goldie, my partner in life and codirector of Chabad of Markham, who has given me the encouragement and words of affirmation needed to complete this book and make my life's dreams a reality;
- My parents Rabbi Shmuel and Devorah Plotkin, for being my role models and guiding lights; my in-laws Rabbi Yisroel and and Mindy Shemtov, for their constant support and confidence; my siblings and my children and grandchildren for just being the best family one can ask for.